BY ANY OTHER NAME

H. Peter Alesso

Novels by
H. Peter Alesso

BY ANY OTHER NAME SAGE
By Any Other Name © 2024
By Any Other Means © 2024
By Any Other Path © 2024

THE HENRY GALLANT SAGA

Midshipman Henry Gallant in Space © 2013
Lieutenant Henry Gallant © 2014
Henry Gallant and the Warrior © 2015
Commander Gallant © 2016
Captain Henry Gallant © 2019
Commodore Henry Gallant © 2020
Henry Gallant and the Great Ship © 2020
Rear Admiral Henry Gallant © 2021
Midshipman Henry Gallant
at the Academy © 2022

Other Novels

Keeper of the Algorithm © 2023
Keeper of the Secret © 2023
Keeper of the Truth © 2023
Captain Hawkins © 2016
Dark Genius © 2017
Youngblood © 2018

Short Story Collection

All Androids Lie © 2022

BY ANY OTHER NAME

H. Peter Alesso
hpeteralesso.com

VSL Publications
Pleasanton, CA 94566

ISBN-13 -
Edition 1.00

SYNOPSIS

*Sometimes, the right man
in the wrong uniform can
make all the difference.*

Ethan, a lowly recruit with an oil-stained uniform and a spirit worn down by disappointment, finds his life forever changed by a twist of fate. Squinting at his reflection, he sees the sleeves of his borrowed jacket bore captain's stripes. A grotesque emblem is embossed over the jacket's breast pocket—a roaring lion's head surrounded by a cluster of jagged broken bones—the symbol of the Special Operations Service.

There is no way out. The ship is taking off because they think an elite SOS captain is on board to take command—him.

His choices were brutally simple . . . act like the officer everyone thought he was or be found out as a fraud. One was survival, the other . . .

The consequences sent a wave of panic through him. He was a mouse in a lion's skin. He had to become that lion until he found a way out of his cage.

Ethan's path intersects with Kate Haliday, the leader of the dark matter project in the Cygni star system. A subtle dance of glances and half-spoken truths begins. But the threads of connection are fragile as they are tangled with the ambitions of Commander Varek, a skeptical officer.

The emergence of an unknown alien race casts a long shadow that shifts the cosmic chessboard of a space fleet and a galactic empire. Their interest in dark matter and Earth's colonies weaves a layer of mystery and suspense.

In this hard science fiction dance, Ethan must navigate the intricacies of love, rivalry, and alien invasion. The possibility of being unveiled darkens his every step. With each move, the line between the man he is and the officer he pretended to be . . . blurs.

∞

Juliet: 'Tis but thy name that is my enemy.
. . . O, be some other name!
What's in a name? That which we call a rose,
by any other name would smell as sweet.

— William Shakespeare's *Romeo and Juliet.*

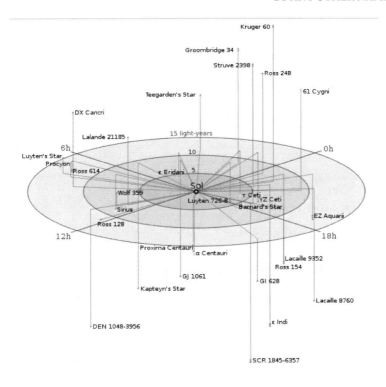

EARTH IMPERIUM—3rd Fleet

Captain Elias Thorne
Spacecraft Carrier - *Orion*
36 Fighters
48 Bombers
6 Recon

Battlecruisers – Invincible, Indominable
12 Cruisers
48 Destroyers
 2 Stealth Recon
12 Auxiliary Support Ship

Sergeant Simpson
2nd Special Operations Services Squad

OV'aa—Battle Fleet

Admiral Zo'axa
 4 Dreadnought
 6 Battlecruisers
 36 Cruisers
 88 Destroyers
 88 Auxiliary Support Ships

CONTENTS

CHAPTER 1

Imitation

The acrid stench of hydraulic fluid filled the tiny compartment, stinging my nostrils and making my eyes water. Hot and stifling panic pulsed in my ears, blurring the dull hum of the starship. The sticky spray of oil from the ruptured valve covered my uniform like a shroud. I frantically sealed the leaking valve and ripped off my offending uniform.

The stink of oil was everywhere. My finger struck the keypad device which boasted a biohazard sensor. I hit the keys over and over again, but it whined with denial.

A red light blinked: CONTAMINATION!

The hatch remained locked.

I threw my grease-stained clothes into the disposal and fumbled in the dimness for replacements in the belongings I was supposed to deliver aboard the *Excalibur*.

This was just one more screw-up, but it had

me picturing my parents' faces. Their flicker of hope extinguished when word reached them back home on that dirt-poor rock of a planet, I was supposed to save them from.

I had to deliver this gear and then vanish before my reputation as a screw-up caught up with me. I pawed through the gear, hunting for a lifeline in the flickering dim red light.

Finally, my fingers snagged on something stiff and formal amidst the softness of civilian attire. I pulled out a uniform, the weight of it surprising in this frantic moment. Shoving my arms into the sleeves, I slipped on the jacket, then the trousers. The pristine fabric soothing against my skin, a foreign sensation. It felt . . . powerful.

Once more, I tried the keypad. Thankfully, this time the lock released, and the hatch opened.

A sliver of light cut across the deck. I swore under my breath and grabbed the gear. Time was a fist pounding at my skull. If caught now, it would be more than the brig—I'd be hauled in for insubordination and destruction of naval property. More and more accusations piled up in my mind.

As I stepped out into the blinding light of the corridor, a junior officer, crisp and formal, snapped to attention in front of me.

I almost dropped the gear.

The lieutenant stammered, "Sir, . . . I'm surprised to see you here so early. The manifest listed your arrival on the next rotation."

Sir?

I froze in disbelief, my heart hammering against my ribcage. A single drop of oil ran down my temple. I nodded stiffly, my throat constricting as if caught in a vice.

The officer's eyes were wide, respectful, with a hint of fear flickering within them. "I'll advise the bridge that you're on board, sir."

His voice was formal, typical of the fleet's discipline, yet there was an undertone of curiosity at this deviation from protocol. He pivoted sharply on his heel and left with a rushed step.

Bewildered, my stomach plummeted a minute later as the loudspeaker crackled to life.

"All hands prepare for immediate launch."

I heard the clang of hatches and the scurry of the crew dashing to their station. Sealed hatches meant no escape. I was trapped!

My blood ran cold as I caught my reflection in the glossy metal bulkhead. Squinting at the image, I saw a ghost. My face, pale above the crisp collar, stared back. The sleeves of my jacket bore captain's stripes. A grotesque emblem was embossed over the jacket's breast pocket. It was a roaring lion's head surrounded by a cluster of jagged broken bones—the symbol of the Special Operations Service.

My mouth turned to sand. Whispers of the SOS's merciless missions danced at the edge of my fraying consciousness, each tale more haunting than the last.

My hands shook as I touched the emblem. There was no way out. The ship was taking off because they thought an elite SOS captain was on board to take command—me.

When they jumped to warp, they would realize this supposed officer wasn't who he seemed to be.

I thought frantically—*there must be a way, just a sliver of time and space to concoct some half-baked escape plan.*

I straightened my new and far too imposing jacket. It sat oddly on my shoulders, the weight of far more than cloth now pressing down on me.

My choices were brutally simple . . . act like the officer everyone thought I was or be found out as a fraud. One was survival, the other . . .

The consequences of the latter sent a fresh wave of panic through me. I was a mouse in a lion's skin. I had to become that lion until I found a way out of this cage.

A wave of dizziness washed over me as I continued down the corridor.

This isn't happening—that internal chant kept looping in my head.

Yet, every step, every crisp salute thrown my way, screamed that it very much was.

I can't think.

That'll be a luxury when I'm imprisoned and have unlimited free time.

My pulse echoed the dread of disappointing my family once more.

"Just don't mess up," were my father's parting words. It was a mantra now twisted into a taunt. A memory flashed—my mother's hopeful smile, fragile as the life we had eked out on our dust-choked planet.

The ship vibrated beneath my feet as the engines roared to life. Like a slumbering beast she awakened in preparation for the ship's departure from the space station. I clutched the officer's belongings tighter, trembling slightly. This farce could end before it even begins. And I had no doubt it would not end well.

I neared the officer's quarters. If they'd been expecting him, someone with authority might be waiting who'd recognize the insignia and... probably not care one bit about the floundering young third-class petty officer hidden beneath it.

Another loudspeaker announcement blared, startling me: "All officers take your stations. Ten minutes to launch."

Ten minutes.

That was my window, a life preserver in this sudden storm. Ten minutes to invent a plan, a backstory for the very essence of an officer I'd spent years wishing to become . . . and failing.

I opened the hatch to the officer's assigned quarters, revealing a compact but well-appointed cabin. Beyond was another hatch likely leading to the bridge. But hesitation, my ever-present companion, froze me in place. I had to find anything to solidify this act before takeoff made it permanent.

My gaze settled on a tablet resting precariously on the edge of the gear I carried. Reports? Mission details? If I could glean some information, I might find a foothold in this world of captains and covert missions. My desperation gave me a surge of boldness. Then, a glimmer of possibility. It was not a mission file but a personal log, access restricted but not impenetrable. My last punishment detail had involved hacking devices like this one, letting me crack the device in a few frantic keystrokes—and I was in.

My fingers flew over the screen. I swiped through what felt like an endless stream of files and jargon. My pulse throbbed in time with the hum of the engines preparing for launch.

A name materialized—Captain Elias Thorne.

Below it, scattered notes. A fondness for a rare tea blend?

That seems strange for a ruthless SOS officer.

There was a coded message about a woman in some far-flung colony. This man, this hardened visage of authority, had fears, preferences . . . cracks in his armor that I might exploit.

The comm unit beeped. I jolted, fumbling the device. A feminine voice, crisp and efficient, echoed in my ears, "Captain Thorne, your presence is required on the bridge. Launch imminent."

"Acknowledged," I barked out, the voice barely my own, roughened with a tension I hoped passed as authority.

I dropped the tablet into my pocket and exited the room with strides I forced to be confident. The corridor was deserted, the ship personnel were busy with their duties.

I reached the bridge, squared my shoulders, smoothed down my too-perfect jacket, and stepped into the ship's epicenter.

The bridge hummed with controlled chaos, a symphony of beeping consoles and urgent chatter. The central viewscreen dominated the room, displaying the sprawling spaceport, its docking bays, and glittering ships as a testament to the vast frontier that awaited them. Screens flickered, and officers barked orders.

My borrowed uniform with its damning lion's head gleaming proudly, drew eyes and silent murmurs.

For the first time, I wondered if anyone knew what the real Thorne looked like.

CHAPTER 2

Launch

"**A**ttention on deck!" shouted a Marine guard. The bridge crew stood like statues frozen in antiquity.

Just as frozen, I remained at the hatch for a long moment.

Finally, I breathed, "As you were."

"Welcome, Captain. I'm Commander Charles Varek, the XO," said a smooth voice, cutting cleanly through the hum of the bridge like a knife through still water.

I stepped onto the bridge deck, finding myself face-to-face with a man whose very bearing commanded attention. His uniform was immaculate, each crease sharp enough to cut, and his posture was so perfect it seemed almost sculpted. He was older, his hair touched a bit of silver, and his sharp gray eyes bore into me, appraising me with a cold, calculating gaze.

In contrast, I stood at six foot two, my athletic build honed by years of physical training. My brown hair, though slightly tousled from the hasty change of uniform, framed a face that was appealing. My hazel eyes, flecked with green and gold, met Varek's steely gaze with a mix of determination and carefully concealed apprehension. Despite the stark difference in our appearances—my youth and vitality against Varek's seasoned austerity—there was an undeniable presence about me. I tried to project an aura of command that seemed to come naturally, even if it was born of necessity rather than true confidence.

"Commander Varek," I acknowledged, striving to inject a note of authority into my voice.

My eyes widened as I sought to drink everything in. I was impressed by the innovative technology. The novelty of my role on this ship was not lost on me.

Varek said, "We should proceed with the change of command ceremony, sir."

I nodded.

Varek recited, "Pursuant to fleet orders, Captain Elias Thorne will assume command of the Earth Imperium ship, *Excalibur*, on this date on the Alpha Centauri Space Station."

He continued reciting more official paragraphs, but from that moment forward, I was officially the commanding officer of the *Excalibur*.

With the formal requirements concluded, I spoke over the address system.

"At ease. Officers and crew of the *Excalibur*, I'm

proud to serve with you. I look forward to getting to know each one of you. For now, we must begin our mission. There are battles to be fought, and the *Excalibur* has a key role to play."

Satisfied with my brief statement, I nodded to Varek.

The bridge crew returned to their launch preparations.

"Five minutes to launch, Captain."

The helmsman's voice cut through the blur of faces on the bridge, drawing my focus.

Five minutes, just enough time to completely unravel.

The *Excalibur* was a state-of-the-at cruiser that weighed 80,000 tons and had a length of 460 meters and a beam of 80 meters. Its armament included four bow missile tubes, two aft missile tubes, ten short-range plasma weapons, forty laser guns amidships, armor belts, and force shields with electronic warfare decoys and sensors. The 1,314 officers and crew were highly trained and used to dealing with the unexpected.

Outside, the vast emptiness of space contrasted with the ship's packed bridge crew crowded into a semicircular hi-tech equipment-packed bridge.

My knowledge of the ship and bridge procedures was rudimentary. I had only witnessed a spaceship launch from remote stations as a petty officer.

I'll have to pull off the bluff of a lifetime to navigate the next few minutes.

I took a moment to survey the concentric circles of equipment. Its efficient layout with the captain's chair in the center allowed for numerous AI and virtual screen resources. The entire bridge was buzzing with personnel preparing for launch, but everyone made way for me as I took my seat.

Various active and passive sensor arrays supplied real-time data to astrophysics. The sensing equipment included different types of active radars and passive telescopes. Every contact tracked had a specific emission signature they could identify. The spectrum of the *Excalibur's* emissions included electromagnetic, Fermion, and dark matter. It was strictly controlled to prevent others from detecting and tracking us.

My gaze flickered across the screens that showed unknown environments, unfamiliar star charts, and tactical readouts my bleary eyes barely comprehended. Behind the facade of command, my thoughts screamed with the same panic as before, just hidden a little better now.

I leaned against a console, the cold metal biting through the borrowed jacket.

"Status check on drive," I said, trying to project an air of authority, by repeating a command I once heard. But my voice rasped like an untuned engine.

"Warp drive stable in hot standby, Captain. Ready to depart the Alpha Centauri space station on your orders," a female voice responded, crisp and formal. A hint of youthful enthusiasm underscored her words.

I subtly slid a hand over a monitor screen, tapping at commands. The ship's roster flickered on the screen. The Officer of the Deck was Lieutenant Ayne Chalamet. The screen's faint glow revealed a young woman with short, raven-black hair and strikingly focused eyes. Even beneath the standard uniform, an air of determination radiated from her. She looked eager to prove herself.

"Proceed," I said, keeping my voice even. I turned my attention to the youngest member on the bridge team, Second Class Petty Officer William Craig, the helmsman. Short and wiry, with a ruddy complexion, he was probably twenty years old—a few years younger than me.

I wondered if he'd ever questioned a captain's orders, or was he blind to the absurdity of a fresh-faced P. O. suddenly becoming an SOS legend?

From their relaxed, casual appearance, they might have seemed blase; yet their eyes showed the keen training of a skilled team. This was a veteran crew from among the best the fleet had to offer, especially picked for this mission. I decided to act as if I had complete confidence in this crew's professional expertise without any micromanagement.

I said, "Proceed."

As the ship slowly moved away from the station, the crew responded to their duties without question. But for me, each beat of my heart felt like a stolen second. I needed a plan. I swiped nervous fingers over the stolen laptop, Thorne's log, and my lifeline.

Where the hell is the real Captain Thorne? Will he suddenly appear, demanding an explanation?

"Ship clear of the station, sir. Ready to accelerate on the designated mission course."

"Proceed."

Minutes passed.

"Sir, all systems are reporting nominal." The OOD again, anticipation sparkling in her voice. "Ready to engage warp drive, sir."

I couldn't delay any longer. Every second, I increased the risk of discovery. I forced myself to meet her eyes and speak the one word that cemented my desperate act.

"Proceed."

I hope that's enough.

The OOD ordered, "Engage warp drive."

"Engaging warp drive," responded the helmsman.

"Communications lost," said the communications officer, making the routine announcement.

I looked at the screen projection of our destination, the Cygni star system.

"Any known anomalies in that sector, Lieutenant?" I barked out the question to the astrogator.

The lieutenant, a weathered man with slick brown hair and callouses on his hands, turned from his console. His gaze met mine with a flicker of experienced deference. "No, sir. It's a backwater system, standard survey, and possible terraforming."

I glanced at the roster on the tactical monitor, Lieutenant Horatio Chen. The name caught me off guard. The file didn't mention his heritage. But there was no time to dwell on that.

Thorne's notes mentioned something about an outpost, a hidden research facility... a strange woman was somehow involved. It was a thread, flimsy and uncertain, but all I had.

"I'd like a full sensor sweep of the fourth planet post-jump. Anomaly scans at maximum sensitivity."

"The fourth planet, sir? It's barely a habitable rock..." the lieutenant began, but I cut him off.

"My orders stand, Lieutenant. And inform the science teams to prepare for immediate planetary resupply upon arrival." I hoped it sounded like a special op with classified objectives, not the desperate hope it indeed was.

The lieutenant responded, "Aye aye, sir."

My deception had bought me the tiniest sliver of time. Now, I clung to that sliver like a drowning man clings to a piece of driftwood. But the ocean was vast, and I couldn't swim forever. I knew that my makeshift raft of lies and half-truths couldn't keep me afloat indefinitely. Sooner or later, waves of suspicion would come crashing down, threatening to drag me beneath the surface.

"OOD, I will be in my cabin. I do not wish to be disturbed until we reach our destination. Is that clear?"

"Yes, sir."

As the ship shuddered and settled into the

rhythm of its journey, I retreated to a shadowy corner of my cabin, the eyes of the crew subtly following me.

I opened Captain Thorne's laptop, scrolling frantically. Images of a young woman's eyes, which held a steely glance, flickered past. Personal notes— fears about her work in some distant world, cryptic lines about needing him.

Images of my family flashed through my mind. Back then, I needed money, a quick way out of the hole our family had sunk into. Now, I just needed a way out of this uniform.

For two days, I tried to hack into the ship's security system to access my mission files and requirements. But they weren't as vulnerable as Thorne's tablet. Finally, in desperation, I called the ship's data security officer, Lieutenant Stamos, who happened to be the young officer I first ran into when I emerged from the airlock.

In an adamant voice, I commanded, "Lieutenant, delete all my biometric and security codes throughout the ship. Replace them with a single 16-digit code that I will enter when you are ready."

The startled officer hemmed and hawed for thirty seconds before he said, "Aye aye, sir."

In ten minutes, I smiled as I gained access to Thorne's most secret and sensitive information. And I had removed the most condemning evidence against me.

Next, I began hunting for answers to what needed to happen when the *Excalibur* reached the top-secret research facility on the fourth planet of Cygni.

I delved into the classified files. I searched for any scrap of information that could help me navigate the treacherous waters ahead. The research facility on Cygni IV loomed like a dark shadow on the horizon, a mystery that could either be my salvation or my undoing. But my thoughts kept returning to a single question.

Why is an SOS captain leading this mission?

During the dreary days in hyperspace, I sat in the confines of my quarters, my heart racing due to the weight of my situation. I kept to my cabin, afraid that my lack of knowledge and inexperience would expose me if I engaged in conversation with the crew. I was a fraud, an imposter thrust into a role I had no right to claim, and the knowledge of my own inadequacy gnawed at me like a festering wound.

With trembling hands, I reached for Thorne's AI neural interface, a sleek, black skullcap lined with a web of delicate connections. I found the device while frantically searching through Thorne's belongings, a desperate man grasping at any strand of hope.

The neural interface was a marvel of modern technology, a tool designed to mentally link to the ship's AI supercomputer. It was an educational tool which fed knowledge and skills directly into the brain through a series of carefully modulated electrical impulses. It was a closely guarded secret of the SOS, a means of rapidly training their operators.

I hesitated to pull the skullcap onto my head.

I thought, *I shouldn't tamper with such a device.*

Then, I winced as I pulled it on. The neural connections contacted my scalp. A tingling sensation spread across my skin, a prickling warmth that seemed to penetrate deep into my skull.

I closed my eyes, and the world fell away.

Quickly, I found myself adrift in a sea of information, a swirling vortex of data and procedure that threatened to overwhelm my senses. The neural educator fed knowledge directly into my mind, allowing me to learn and comprehend at a rapid rate. I directed my thoughts to ask questions.

I saw schematics of the *Excalibur's* engines, intricate diagrams that laid bare the secrets of the ship's propulsion systems. I witnessed the destructive power of the vessel's weapons, from the searing heat of the plasma cannons to the devastating impact of the fusion missiles.

Combat tactics unfolded before my mind's eye, a dizzying array of maneuvers and countermeasures designed to outthink and outfight any adversary. I absorbed the principles of leadership, the art of inspiring and directing men and women in the heat of battle.

The knowledge came in a relentless torrent, a flood of information that would have taken years to acquire through traditional means. My mind reeled under the onslaught, my synapses firing in rapid succession as they struggled to accommodate the influx of data.

When the flood of information finally subsided, I found myself gasping for breath, my body drenched in sweat and my mind afire with newfound knowledge. I tore the skullcap from my head, my hands shaking as I struggled to process the enormity of what had just transpired.

My head aches! I need to rest.

I took frequent breaks from the neural device to allow myself to reflect on what I learned and to see if I was remembering as much as possible. Though I had frightful headaches from the device, I kept at it day after day. Each day I tried to expand my expertise and abilities to fulfill the role I had to play.

The journey through hyperspace was longer than I expected. It proved enough time for me to develop a routine for eating, studying, and sleeping. There was little else to do since I had standing orders not to be disturbed unless it was an emergency.

I'll keep my fingers crossed that there are no emergencies.

Time lost all meaning as I drowned in the sea of information, my sense of self slowly eroding under the weight of the neural educator's relentless instruction. I became a vessel, a conduit for the skills and expertise of a thousand SOS operatives who had come before me.

Over time I began to gain confidence that I could navigate through the maze of requirements of a ship's captain, but the role of Elias Thorne remained mysterious.

The headaches were a problem, and I was forced

to take pain medication periodically.

I knew now, with some clarity, the intricacies of the *Excalibur's* systems, the strengths and weaknesses of her crew, and the tactics that would be required against any foe.

I can visualize the ship's systems.

But the knowledge alone, as vast and comprehensive as it was, was not enough. I knew that the true test of my newfound skills would come not in the sterile confines of my quarters, but in the crucible of actual operations and combat.

I would have to be the man to wield this knowledge, to apply it with the resolute determination and unwavering courage that the crew of the *Excalibur* deserved from their captain.

I rose to my feet, my body still trembling from the aftershocks of the neural education. I caught a glimpse of myself in the mirror, and for a moment, I hardly recognized the man staring back at me.

Will it be enough?

CHAPTER 3

Collision Course

"Warp bubble collapsed, sir," helmsman Craig reported, his voice steady amidst the hum of the bridge.

The *Excalibur* dropped smoothly out of warp. As the intricate operation ended, the ship shuddered almost imperceptibly.

The subtle changes to the surrounding space-time fabric were inconspicuous to the crew. Nevertheless, I could feel a subtle difference beneath my feet to the ship's rhythmic vibrations.

The bridge crew's placid response to the event prompted me to strike a similar blasé pose. I stood on the bridge, the vast space unfolding on the main screen. The crew buzzed with post-jump checks.

Cygni 61 was a binary star system in the constellation Cygnus. It consisted of a pair of K-type dwarf stars that orbited each other in a period of about 659 years. The dual stars' radiance drew the

Excalibur deeper into their gravity well. The ship's forward viewport revealed the stars' inner fusion turmoil as they converted vast amounts of hydrogen to helium.

"Ahead standard," I ordered, getting comfortable with the newly acquired knowledge I gained with the neural training.

"Aye, aye, sir," said Craig. He alerted engineering to adjust the sub-light antimatter fusion reactors.

"Nicely done, Helm," I commented a few seconds later.

Master Chief Petty Officer Jacob "the Fixer" Kovalenko ran through the post checkoff list. He had a compact build but exuded wiry strength. Short, buzzed hair the color of tarnished copper rested over his penetrating brown eyes, which seemed to assess problems with a glance. A network of faded but intricate scars crisscrossed his right forearm, hinting at a hard-fought past. Practical and efficient to a fault, he spoke bluntly, "All stations nominal, Captain."

"Very well," I said.

The astrogator reported, "Sir, we're two light-days from the fourth planet. There are five planets visible. The first is designated Cygni-Alpha and has an orbital radius of thirty million kilometers. Spectral analysis shows it's a composite of a carbonaceous, silicate, and metal-rich rock covering a barren volcanic mantle."

The planet's radio telescope image offered me exciting views.

"No moons," commented the master chief. His

uniform's well-creased trousers and mirror-glossed shoes reflected his pride.

"I'm only interested in the fourth planet," I said.

"The fourth planet, designated Cygni-Gamma, has a 121-million-kilometer orbit. It's a warm-water planet, Earth-type in size and general character, sir," continued the astrogator.

"With one large moon," contributed Chief Kovalenko.

"The other planets are gas giants with no moons. The last planet follows a small asteroid field with a 344-million-kilometer orbit, sir."

"Very well," I acknowledged. "Cygni-Gamma is called Janus. That's our destination and where the research facility is located."

As the ship came into orbit over the fourth planet two days later, Kovalenko said, "Captain, the head of the physics research facility on Janus is signaling."

I nodded, steeling myself for yet another performance. The screen came alive, and Dr. Kate Haliday appeared. Her compact frame radiated restless energy, her eyes a startling hazel green. The standard lab coat she wore didn't hide the determination in her posture. Nor could her hastily pinned hair conceal the brilliance in her gaze as she appeared on the screen.

"Captain," she began her voice carrying the confidence of someone used to being the smartest person in the room. "I need to discuss the parameters of Project Janus. My work here requires certain ...

freedoms that I'm not sure military protocol realizes."

I met her gaze, noting the spark of challenge flickering behind her directness. "Dr. Haliday, I'm aware of the importance of your research. But you're under my command now, and the success of this mission depends on discipline and order."

Her eyebrows shot up, a mixture of surprise and irritation flashing across her features. "With all due respect, Captain, you're a military man. What do you know about theoretical physics or harnessing dark matter? My team and I need the liberty to explore unconventional avenues without being hamstrung by red tape."

I felt an edge of frustration creeping into my voice. "And you must understand that this is a military mission, not a university laboratory. Your 'unconventional avenues' can't compromise the safety of this ship or its mission."

The standoff lasted a moment longer before Kate's expression softened slightly, her pragmatic side coming to the fore. "Look, Captain, I'm not one to step on toes, but I wonder why the Navy sent an elite special forces captain to this station?"

I wonder the same thing.

I said, "The navy has its reasons."

Kate looked disconcerted but continued, "I want to ensure we're not wasting time. Or worse, missing out on breakthroughs because we're too afraid to follow the opportunities."

I saw the passion behind her words and the genuine drive to push the boundaries of science. It was a trait I could respect, even admire. "Alright, Dr. Haliday. We'll work together on this. But it must be a two-way street. You keep me informed, and I'll ensure you have the flexibility you need . . . within reason."

Kate considered me for a moment as if weighing my sincerity. Finally, she said, "Deal, Captain. Please visit our planet so I can show you our facilities and what we are accomplishing. Let's make history, shall we?"

I couldn't help but feel the weight of my charade pressing down on me. Here was a woman dedicating her life to the pursuit of knowledge, and I was nothing but a pretender in a stolen uniform.

As the small craft descended towards Janus, I found myself mesmerized by the planet's unique beauty. The craft shuddered as it broke through the swirling bands of jade and crimson that colored the upper atmosphere. Below revealed a landscape that seemed to meet earthly norms. Rust-red mountains stretched out before me. The jagged edges softened by the ethereal light that filtered through the clouds. Vast oceans shimmering with an otherworldly iridescence. They lapped at the shores of well-developed vegetation that clung tenaciously to the rocky soil.

The research facility itself was a stark contrast to the landscape. Its geometric lines and gleaming metal surfaces were located on the outskirts of a small town where the scientists and their families lived.

As the craft touched down on the landing pad, I felt a mix of excitement and trepidation course through me. This was it, the moment I had been both anticipating and dreading. I was about to step into the heart of Project Janus. The cutting-edge scientific endeavor held the key to unlocking the secrets and the mission that an SOS captain was sent to command.

Kate was already waiting for me, her lab coat fluttering in the gentle breeze. She greeted me with a nod, her eyes still holding a hint of the earlier challenge. "Welcome to Janus, Captain," she said, her voice crisp and professional. "I trust you'll find our facilities to your satisfaction."

I returned the nod, my own expression neutral. "I'm sure I will, Dr. Haliday. Shall we?"

Together, we made our way into the main research building, our footsteps echoing in the cavernous hallways. As we walked, Kate began to explain the intricacies of the project, her passion for her work evident in every word.

"We've made significant strides in our understanding of dark matter," she said, her eyes gleaming with excitement. "The unique properties of Janus, its position in the binary star system, and the unusual energy fluctuations we've detected... it all points to this being the perfect place to conduct our experiments."

I listened intently, trying to absorb Kate's scientific concepts. I may have been playing the role of a seasoned captain, but in truth, I felt like a first-year midshipman struggling to keep up. The more Kate talked, the more I realized just how much I had to learn.

As we entered the main laboratory, I was struck by the sheer scale of the operation. Massive machines hummed and whirred, their purposes beyond my comprehension. Scientists in white coats scurried about, their faces a mix of concentration and excitement. In the center of it all stood a towering structure, its sleek lines and pulsing energy field suggesting a technology far beyond anything I had ever seen.

"That's our dark matter reactor," Kate explained, noticing my gaze. "It's the heart of our operation."

I nodded, trying to look like I understood. In truth, I was feeling more and more out of my depth with each passing moment. Here I was, a fraud in a captain's uniform, surrounded by some of the brightest minds in the galaxy.

How long can I keep up this charade?

As if sensing my unease, Kate turned to me, her expression softening slightly. "I know this must all be a bit overwhelming, Captain," she said, her voice almost gentle. "But trust me when I say that what we're doing here has the potential to change everything—a potential source of limitless energy."

I met her gaze. At that moment, I felt something stir within me—a desire to be a part of something greater, to contribute to a cause beyond my selfish needs and wishes.

"I do trust you, Dr. Haliday," I said, surprising myself with honesty in my words. "And I want to support your work in any way I can. Even if I don't fully understand it."

Kate smiled then, a genuine smile that lit up her face. "Thank you, Captain. That means a lot."

She thought, maybe he'll be flexible.

For the first time, she relaxed and felt a genuine sense of friendship.

As the day wore on, we found ourselves standing on an observation deck, looking out at the landscape. The sky had transformed into a kaleidoscope of celestial colors, dancing and blending above us like an otherworldly aurora.

"It's beautiful, isn't it?" Kate murmured.

I nodded, feeling a sense of awe wash over me. At that moment, standing beside this brilliant woman, gazing out at a world unlike anything I had ever seen, I felt a flicker of something I hadn't experienced in a long time. A sense of purpose, of belonging.

I knew I was still an imposter, but maybe, just maybe, I could become something more. Perhaps this mission, this place, these people... maybe they could help me find the truth about myself.

"It is," I said softly, my voice almost lost in the gentle breeze. "Let's hope it holds the answers we're both looking for."

The next day, Kate strolled across the stone walkway, in the middle of the town's garden park. Its centrally located water fountain glistened under the late summer sun. Everyone who passed greeted her warmly—for she was well-respected to the people of Janus. Yet, it wasn't her eye-catching yellow dress, or her radiant vitality, that captured the attention of those around her. Nor was it her long, rich golden-brown hair, green eyes, and soft skin. No, what was most striking was her bearing—shoulders back, head high. It begged the question 'what adventure is she undertaking now?'

When I saw her, my reaction was unlike what might be expected from a methodical, logical captain.

I was flustered.

And as her shoes struck the stone footpath, the sound drew my attention.

For the first time, I realized how attractive she was.

When she noticed me, she turned.

Passersby might assume that we were acquaintances meeting casually, but unexpectedly, my heart was pounding, and my palms were sweaty.

"Captain, let me show you around our little academic community," Kate said with a warm smile. "There are about 3,000 inhabitants, including scientists, staff, engineers, their families, and the support people. We have established a happy prosperous community in this far-flung world."

As we walked side by side, I couldn't help but marvel at the quaint charm of the town. It had an air of idyllic tranquility, with its neat rows of houses, each adorned with well-tended gardens and colorful window boxes. Children's laughter echoed from a nearby playground, and the occasional hum of a hovering transport added a touch to an otherwise timeless Earth scene.

Kate pointed out various landmarks as we strolled, her enthusiasm for the community evident in every word. "Over there is the research complex," she said, gesturing to a sleek, modern building at the edge of town. "It's the heart of our work here on Janus."

I nodded, my gaze lingering on the complex for a moment before turning back to Kate. "And the people of Newville, are they're all dedicated to this mission?"

"Absolutely," Kate replied, her eyes shining with pride. "Everyone in Newville has made sacrifices to be a part of this endeavor. They've left behind friends, and the comforts of Earth to pursue something greater. It's a testament to the human spirit, don't you think?"

I couldn't help but agree. As we continued our walk, I found myself drawn into the rhythm of life on Janus. We passed a bustling market square, where vendors hawked exotic fruits and handcrafted wares. The air was filled with the rich aromas of sizzling street food and the chatter.

Kate led me to a small café nestled between a bookshop and a tech repair store. The sign above the door read "The Quantum Leap" in glowing holographic letters. Inside, the café was a cozy haven, with plush armchairs, shelves lined with well-thumbed books, and the rich scent of freshly brewed coffee.

As we settled into a quiet corner, Kate ordered us each a slice of decadent chocolate cake and a steaming mug of the café's signature blend.

On an impulse, I asked, "Do you have yellow chamomile tea?"

It was the rare blend of tea that I had found in Thorne's log.

To my surprise, the waitress stared at me for a full minute, then she looked at the roaring lion's head emblem of my beast. She left abruptly but soon returned with the brew.

I couldn't remember the last time I'd indulged in such simple pleasures, and I found myself savoring every bite and sip.

Over our impromptu snack, Kate regaled me with stories of Janus' early days, of the challenges and triumphs that had shaped the community into what it was today. I listened intently, marveling at the resilience and ingenuity of these pioneers who had carved out a home on the edge of the unknown.

As the afternoon wore on, I found myself increasingly drawn to Kate's infectious enthusiasm and keen intellect. Our conversation flowed effortlessly, ranging from the intricacies of research to the implications of humanity's expansion.

It was only when the café's owner politely informed us that she was closing for the evening that

I realized how much time had passed.

As we got up to leave, the café owner came to me. She said, "Please take this for your personal use."

It was a bag of rare yellow chamomile tea.

She said, "And please let me know if there is anything else I could do for you."

I stared at the owner as I took the gift.

As Kate and I stepped out into the cool evening air, the stars of the Cygni system twinkled.

Kate turned to me. "Thank you for today, Captain," she said softly. "It's been a long time since I've had the chance to share my love for Newville with someone who could appreciate it."

I felt a warmth spread through my chest, a feeling I hadn't experienced in longer than I could remember. "The pleasure was all mine," I replied, my voice low and earnest. "You've shown me a side of Janus, and of yourself, that I appreciate."

As we parted ways, I found myself already looking forward to our next encounter. Kate had awakened something within me, a sense of wonder and possibility.

And as I made my way back to the Excalibur, the weight of my mission and the challenges ahead seemed just a little bit lighter.

But in the back of my mind, I wondered . . . *why yellow chamomile tea.*

CHAPTER 4

Ship Shape

As I settled into my new role as Captain Elias Thorne, I quickly realized that the knowledge gained from the AI neural educator was only the beginning of my journey. The sheer complexity of the Excalibur's systems and the weight of command were far more daunting than I had anticipated.

I decided to patrol the space between the inner planets to gain some elementary ship handling experience. I found myself surrounded by a flurry of activity, with crew members reporting status updates and seeking my guidance. The terminology and protocols felt foreign on my tongue, and I often stumbled over my words, drawing curious glances from my subordinates.

"Captain, the navigational array is showing a slight deviation from our plotted course," Lieutenant Chen reported, his brow furrowed as he studied the holographic display.

I felt a surge of panic rise in my chest. The

neural educator had provided me with a theoretical understanding of astronavigation but applying that knowledge in real-time was proving to be a challenge.

"I... let me see," I stammered, moving to Chen's station, and staring at the complex readouts. My mind raced as I tried to recall the procedures for course correction, but the information seemed to slip through my grasp like sand through my fingers.

Varek, ever observant, stepped in smoothly. "If I may, Captain," he said, his tone carefully neutral. "A minor adjustment to our bearing should suffice. Shall I instruct the helmsman to make the necessary corrections?"

I felt a flush of embarrassment creep up my neck, but I nodded gratefully. "Yes, Commander. Make it so."

As Varek relayed the orders, I couldn't shake the feeling that I was out of my depth. The crew's efficiency and expertise only served to highlight my own inadequacies, and I wondered how long I could maintain the charade.

In the days that followed, I threw myself into my responsibilities with a determination born of desperation. I spent long hours in my quarters, poring over technical manuals and ship logs, trying to absorb every scrap of knowledge I could.

I sought out Chief Kovalenko, the grizzled engineer who knew the *Excalibur's* systems better than anyone. Under the guise of inspections and casual conversations, I peppered the chief with questions, soaking up his wisdom and experience like a sponge.

"You see, Captain," Kovalenko explained, his hands gesturing animatedly as we walked through the humming engine room, "the key to keeping a ship like this running smoothly is understanding how all the parts work together. It's not just about procedures; it's about developing a feel for the vessel, a sixth sense for when something's not quite right."

On the busy *Excalibur* bridge, Midshipman Angelica Nicole was one of those vying for my attention. She was the youngest officer, fresh out of the academy. Quick-witted with a disarming grin and dimples to match. In addition, she had a habit of wrinkling her nose when she laughed, which drew attention to her cute face. As tradition dictated, the ship assigned the most junior officer to head the communications division.

As communications officer, Nicole handed me a message tablet with information from Kate Haliday about the progress of updating equipment. Scanning it, I checked off my receipt. I glanced around the bridge at the various consoles to verify that all conditions were satisfactory.

"Mr. Varek," I said.

"Sir?"

"You may relieve the watch."

"Aye aye, sir."

I was satisfied that everything was in order, and

it dawned on me that it would be appropriate for me to walk through the ship to see how the crew was reacting to their new circumstance.

"Mr. Varek, I'm going on a brief walk-through of engineering."

"Yes, sir," said Varek. "Sir, navigation shows some shipping alterations may be needed to transport the remaining scientific equipment to the planet. Request permission to adjust as required?"

I looked over the plot and said, "Permission granted. The OOD has the conn."

With that, I vacated my command chair and left the bridge, heading first for my cabin a dozen steps away. The cabin served alternatively as a sanctuary and an isolation cell. It had a bed, a desk, and a single cabinet, which proved to be enough. Looking around, I remembered the miniature quarters I had as an ordinary spaceman.

This is better.

Over the ship's address system, I heard, "Now set the midday watch; section one. Now set the midday watch; section one."

Then, I went to explore the ship.

The ship was divided into three main compartments: bow, mid-ship, and aft. The bow compartment housed the ship's sensor arrays, weapons systems, and stealth technology. The mid-ship compartment, called the operations compartment, was composed of three decks. It included the bridge and CIC on the upper deck, the wardroom on the second deck, and the crew's living quarters on the third deck. The aft compartment housed the engineering spaces, including the sub-light and FTL engines as well as the hangar bay for small craft.

Running and maintaining an advanced ship was a huge job for the crew. Considerable automation was used throughout, but controls could not be reliably left for AI and machines alone. Much still required human understanding and touch.

As I walked, I could feel the ship activity around me, the crew moving with purpose and determination. They were the lifeblood of the *Excalibur*, the human touch that no machine could replace, and I felt a swell of pride.

Ahead, the broad form of Master Chief Kovalenko came into view, his jaunty walk a testament to his years in various gravity wells.

"Good morning, sir," he called out, his voice a deep rumble that seemed to come from the very heart of the ship.

I smiled, falling into step beside the veteran. "Good morning, Chief."

My confidence in my knowledge of the ship, its systems, and operations had grown sufficiently that I felt I could converse with the chief without giving myself away.

"How's your engine room?" I asked.

"Well," Kovalenko said, "over the past week, just when I got everything exactly the way I like it, the XO held a surprise inspection. Now I must rearrange everything, so that he likes it."

I smiled and said, "That's his job, but I doubt he'll discover that you've missed a trick. I'm sure everything will find its way back to your satisfaction before long."

Kovalenko nodded: "Thank you, sir. Engineering is gathering information on our last hyperspace jump now, but the issues seem to be mostly minor adjustments. A few pieces of equipment have failed, but they're easily replaced."

"Good. Good."

I returned to the bridge in time to see the last shipments of equipment being sent to the planet.

"Request permission to conduct scheduled exercises, sir," asked Varek.

"Permission granted," I said.

The scheduled drills included man-overboard, loss of steering, loss of propulsion, loss of reactor control, fire, and hull rupture.

The initial drills involved simple adjustment in orbit under emergency conditions. After several hours, I allowed the second series of more stressful tests to begin, including depressurizing and repressurizing of compartments to check the hull integrity of the ship.

Toward the end of the day, we evaluated the stealth technology and the *Excalibur's* ability to penetrate enemy defenses and evade detection. A drone was deployed with a sensor array to find and track the *Excalibur* when she was in stealth mode. The stealth technology was based upon an anti-matter superconductor that created a confinement field to cloak the ship. It required several minutes to energize and activate. The time required to enter and leave stealth mode was noted.

Finally, we began exercising the small craft onboard, an ordinary two-man Firebird flyer.

"Skipper," Varek said, "I'd like to suggest that we hold a shooting competition. We could award a marksmanship badge to the battery with the best firing score."

I smiled and said, "I like that idea, XO. Set it up for tomorrow. A little competition would be a great way to stimulate some friendly rivalry."

The next day, when weapons personnel were stationed, the day's drills began.

"Prepare to launch the target drone," I said.

"Aye aye, sir," said Kovalenko at the bridge control console. A remote-controlled drone was released to act as a target.

As the drone flew, the laser fired a direct hit, vaporizing it.

They released another drone.

Next, they fired a missile that hit the drone.

This was followed by a series of plasma and laser target exercises until suddenly a loud alarm sounded . . .

CLANG! CLANG! CLANG!

A series of emergency messages blared from the AI system: "Explosion in the engineering compartment! Fire! Damage control party, proceed immediately to the casualty! This is not a drill!"

The ship's emergency teams sprang into action.

I turned to the junior officer of the watch: "Midshipman Nicole, take charge of the damage control party in the engineering compartment. Report the status of the casualty as soon as you get there."

"Aye aye, sir.

A few minutes later, Nicole reported, "Bridge, DC. I've reached the fire. My team is in fire protective gear and breathing apparatus. Chief Kovalenko has reported that the team is ready. We're entering the compartment."

I was gratified to hear Nicole speak in a relaxed, confident voice.

The overhead fire suppressant system spewed out chemical material to dampen the fire, while automatic hatch closures isolated.

Nicole and the DC team entered the compartment and were immediately engulfed in smoke.

"Kill all the electrical panels!" Nicole ordered, "Close port side isolation valves!"

She evacuated unnecessary personnel.

After several minutes of hazardous work, Nicole reported, "Bridge, DC. The fire is out. Two men have been evacuated to sick bay with burns and smoke inhalation."

Nicole returned to the bridge where I acknowledged her performance with a frank, "Well done."

Later in the wardroom, the officers jostled Nicole with good-natured congratulations.

The next day, I went to Janus to evaluate the progress being made on delivering the experiment equipment.

The transition from the cramped, utilitarian quarters of the ship to the planet was like stepping into another world. The research facility sprawled before me, a vast tiered expanse bathed in the soft glow of numerous screens and panels.

The constant low buzz of activity was the soundtrack of the instruments, a testament to the research team's practiced ease. They moved with a precision and confidence that spoke of countless hours of training.

In this hive of activity, I was an anomaly. The team gave me only cursory glances, their expressions a mix of deference and curiosity.

I said, "Commander Varek, has all of the scientific equipment been delivered planet-side."

"It has, sir."

"Very well. Set up a command post with a defensive perimeter."

Varek said, "I've already made all the preparations. Defensive batteries will be in place tonight," his tone conveying both respect and a hint of something else—something unreadable.

He said, "Captain, I would like to speak to you about something that has concerned me for some time."

I furrowed my brow. "Speak freely."

"On Alpha Centauri, I was under the impression that Captain Thorne was... indisposed and that this mission would be delayed. Yet, you surprisingly appeared at the space station even earlier than expected," Varek said, barely above a whisper. His tone was meticulously polite, but it masked a deeper scrutiny, a probing beneath the surface of my hastily constructed facade.

"A last-minute change of plans," I replied, keeping my response deliberately vague, my voice steady.

"Indeed." Varek's gaze drifted over me with an experienced eye. "We were under orders to take off immediately upon your arrival, so I didn't have an opportunity for any pleasantries . . . until now."

I gave him a cold stare as I rubbed my temple. A headache was coming on and I wanted to get my pills.

"Our men and women," Varek continued, his voice taking on a weightier timbre, "trust in the chain of command. It is disturbing..." He paused, the word 'disturbing' hanging in the air, imbued with a gravity that belied its simplicity, "...having that faith so casually rearranged."

I felt a stab of annoyance spark within me. "We were under a time constraint," I countered, surprised at the firmness of my voice.

"Yet, you arrived without a squad of your

famous Meateaters as an escort."

"I don't appreciate the use of that derogatory slang term when referring to the SOS," I replied with a snarl. Now the word 'Meateaters' hung in the air, a grim reminder of the unit's fearsome reputation.

They were the Imperium's most elite soldiers, known for their ruthlessness and unquestioning loyalty. Whispers of their deeds, of entire colonies brought to heel through fear and force, had become legend. I knew the power of that legend, knew the weight it carried. "My qualifications are in the mission files. I assume you've read them?"

There was a moment of heavy charged silence as Varek's gaze remained fixed on me, unblinking and unreadable.

"Perhaps you missed the addendum," I said. The words tasted bitter. The lie chafed against my conscience like coarse fabric. "There's... sensitivity there, Commander. A need-to-know basis about this mission, these facilities, and these scientists. Your responsibility is the security of these facilities. Leave the mission objects and results to me."

The lie settled between us, a tangible presence. I had never played so brazenly for such high stakes before. I was aware of my peril.

Varek's expression remained impassive before he gave a curt nod, a gesture that seemed to concede the point, albeit reluctantly.

"As you say, Captain. But be mindful," Varek added, his voice lowering, a note of caution threading through his words, "This mission has begun with...

irregularities."

That word too, hung between us, unspoken implications swirling in its wake like dust from the distant past. A troubled history.

In this 22nd century, Earth had been a husk of its former self, its resources depleted, and its people desperate. The discovery of faster-than-light travel had been a lifeline, a promise of salvation in the vast expanse of the cosmos. Mega-corporations, driven by an insatiable hunger for wealth and power, had raced to stake their claims in distant worlds.

But the promise of the stars had come at a cost. Decades of cutthroat competition and corporate wars had left the colonies fractured and vulnerable. In this chaos, Augustus Vitali, a visionary leader with a silver tongue and an iron fist, had risen to prominence. With a blend of charismatic rhetoric and military might, he had forged the warring factions into a powerful alliance—the birth of the Earth Imperium.

Under the rule of Augustus's descendants, the Imperium had embarked on a relentless campaign of expansion. Advanced technology and disciplined legions had brought entire systems to heel. Some welcomed the stability and prosperity of imperial rule, while others had been crushed beneath the boots of conquest by the Special Operation Service.

And now, we were on the edge of the known universe, chasing whispers of dark matter and mysterious happenings. I couldn't help but wonder if this mission was just another chapter in the Imperium's never-ending quest for dominance.

Or was something more at stake that even the mighty Imperium couldn't control?

CHAPTER 5

Piranha

In the vast, inky canvas of space, amidst the swirling galaxies and the piercing lights of distant stars, was a silence so profound it seemed to speak. Here, the Observers of the Void, tall ethereal beings, drifted through the cosmos. Their grey forms and shimmering luminescent eyes mirrored the mysteries of the universe.

They wandered the expanse drawing to the enigmas that elude other civilizations. Their current focus was on the vicinity of the Cygni star system, a region pulsating with rare, elusive dark matter fields.

Their technology was attuned to an anomaly outside the Cygni system. Here, the fabric of space-time danced to an unseen rhythm, a pattern of dark matter that beckoned with an irresistible call.

Though invisible to telescopes, they inferred dark matter's existence through its undeniable gravitational influence within the galaxy's rotation. The OV'aa found surprisingly rapid outer star velocities, implying much more mass must be present than was seen.

The OV'aa looked for massive galaxy clusters that distorted the light of objects behind them, an effect called gravitational lensing. The most dramatic lensing effects were seen far way in the cluster ESO 325-G004 (which was 450 million light-years away). However, much closer stars such as Cygni also experienced weak lensing.

They were aware, however, that they were not alone in their quest.

Humans, a species of boundless curiosity and relentless determination, ventured near this cosmic ballet. The ships of the OV'aa, invisible to the rudimentary sensors of humans, hovered at the edge of perception. They observed, unseen, as humans grappled with the mysteries that the OV'aa had long since unraveled. Yet, there was purity in the humans' quest. Their raw need to understand.

The presence of the OV'aa in the Cygni system was not necessarily an act of aggression but one of observation. They were the chroniclers, the silent witnesses. Humans, with their fleeting lives and boundless dreams, were just the latest chapter.

As the OV'aa drifted through the dark matter currents, they contemplated their next move.

They had entered conflict before. It was a recurring rhythm of civilizations. But there was something ... different ... in this species, a flicker of curiosity beyond pure survival.

For now, the OV'aa waited. Their ships cloaked

in the darkness between the stars. Their eyes fixed on the bustling activity of the Cygni research station.

CHAPTER 6

Paranoia

I stepped into the heart of the Janus research lab. The sterile walls and gleaming equipment starkly contrasted with the rough-and-tumble military world of the Excalibur. I felt a pang of unease, knowing how misplaced my assumed confidence appeared in this realm.

Kate was there, as always, at the center of it all. Her rich golden-brown hair was tied in a ponytail which was askew. Yet, her green eyes held that same intense fire, a blazing determination that made her seem fierce yet fragile.

Her colleague, Dr. Austin Harrison, stood quietly off to one side inspecting equipment. Tall and lean, he had a shock of perpetually messy white hair that seemed at odds with his meticulously pressed lab coat. His eyes twinkled behind wire-rimmed glasses, glowing with boundless curiosity. A walking encyclopedia with endless enthusiasm, he was always quick with a wide smile and a self-deprecating joke.

He once worked with Kate's father when the town and research facility was first founded years earlier.

"Well, Captain?" Kate asked, her voice a sharp contrast to the low hum of the machines. "I hope you haven't come to tell me we're shutting this whole thing down before it even starts."

"I'm not here to do that," I chuckled, wishing the words felt more solid, less like a flimsy shield. "Has all your equipment been delivered and installed?"

"Yes. We're finishing the final system checks and upgrades today," she finished with, "hopefully," with a smile and crossed fingers.

"Good," I said. "But I have some questions about procedures and the expected energy output you hope to achieve."

Her expression shifted from pleasant to something approaching guarded.

I had a tiny jolt of satisfaction that beneath the mask of the brilliant scientist, she too, was affected by my assumed authority. I clung to that feeling, letting it bolster my next words. "Let's talk logistics. I need to understand the risks and rewards involved with this…" I gestured vaguely at the banks of flickering monitors and strange, pulsing machinery "… whole operation."

Her prickliness melted into a begrudging respect. "Finally! Someone who recognizes this isn't some oversized chemistry set." She gestured for me to follow as she moved impatiently to a massive central console.

"Walk me through it. In layman's terms," I said,

trying to sound like the no-nonsense Captain Thorne might.

She was in her element, talking about big machines and bigger science.

She said, "I've theorized a stable Eclipsion particle to account for the observed amount of dark matter in the universe. It produces complex mathematics and physics beyond the Standard Model."

She spoke, and the words washed over me —quantum field generators, dark matter plasma density, fuzzy probability vectors. It was incomprehensible, a symphony of a language I didn't speak. I nodded, furrowed my brow, and pretended those gestures were filled with genuine understanding.

My thoughts drifted back to the laptop in my quarters, Thorne's logs. It mentioned a woman.

Is it Kate?

I snapped back to the present at Kate's voice, hitting a note of exasperation. "...and that's where it gets a bit sticky, if you pardon the pun."

"Sticky, how?" I managed to ask, scrambling to cover my lapse of attention.

She said, "Eclipsion particles are related to SUSY gravitinos that have a spin of $3/2$ and interact weakly with other matter, primarily through gravity."

Harrison came forward and said, "We speculate that Eclipsion particles interact not just with ordinary matter but also with dark energy, this could introduce a dynamic equilibrium in the expansion of the universe."

I furrowed my brow.

"Theoretically, we should be able to nudge dark matter particles into alignment, creating a conduit. But stabilizing anything with that density...well, think of throwing a pebble into an ocean. It's chaos, but controlled chaos...hopefully." Harrison paused, his eyes narrowing. "You're staring at me like a deer in the headlights, Captain. Are you following a single word?"

I forced a smile that felt more like a grimace. "Let's say I'm getting the broad strokes. What happens if this...controlled chaos... gets a bit less controlled?"

Kate hesitated before adding, "We don't fully know. It's why we're here and not in Earth orbit. Could be a small, localized anomaly, could be—" She cut herself off, her voice betraying a fear she struggled to conceal. "The worst-case scenario... it could tear open . . . a temporary... singularity."

"A blackhole?" I supplied.

She nodded grimly.

"Something like it. That's why my team insists on running limited control tests first. But the Department of Energy keeps pushing for results, and frankly, I'm getting desperate." There was a vulnerability in that confession, a crack in her carefully assembled facade of scientific detachment.

For the first time since a twist of fate thrust me into the role of Captain Thorne, I felt something shift inside of me. It wasn't just fear for myself, but the realization there were real stakes here, a danger far beyond my messy charade.

"You're not just chasing some publication here," I said quietly, almost to myself.

She looked at me then, a flicker of surprise and something less guarded in her gaze. "It's the chance for a major breakthrough in physics, Captain. A change in our fundamental understanding of the universe," she whispered, her voice tinged with awe. "Imagine what we might learn, what we could build if we could truly understand, truly harness, dark matter."

At that moment, staring back at her, I saw something of myself—that flicker of ambition, the desperation to prove I could be more than my origin. Suddenly, it felt impossible to let her down, knowing it could put more than just my neck on the line.

I couldn't be Thorne, but perhaps I didn't have to be. Maybe there was another way to survive in Kate's world—if I could find my place there.

"Tell me," I began, my voice finding a new weight. "What can I do to help?"

"You can start by calling me Kate."

"Eth...," I started and then finished, "Elias."

CHAPTER 7

Sparkle

"I enjoyed touring your research facilities," I said.

"I'm glad," said Kate.

"It gives me the chance to return the favor by showing off *Excalibur*," I said with pride.

"I'm looking forward to learning everything I can about your world," she laughed.

The sparkle of *Excalibur's* corridors extended before us. The labyrinth of polished chrome and machinery contrasted the experimental clutter of Kate's facility.

"Military efficiency," I quipped. "Not always known for comfort, but always functional."

Kate's answering smile held a hint of amusement. "Efficiency has its merits. But even with an unlimited budget, every second in a lab feels wasted if it's not spent running a test or crunching data. That takes priority over neatness."

"Then I hope you'll appreciate that a well-maintained ship has a beauty of its own," I countered. I gestured towards a viewport where the swirl of the Cygni system painted an abstract masterpiece against the backdrop of space.

"A beauty that's essential to survival," she conceded. "It's easy to forget how fragile we are in space. For all its cutting-edge equipment, Janus still feels like a glorified village compared to this." She tapped a fingertip against the reinforced glass viewport.

"Indeed, it is," I agreed, my respect for her growing. Her awe for the cosmos was genuine.

The tour moved through engineering, a pulsating heart of plasma conduits, and humming nuclear antimatter reactors. Kate paused by a particularly intricate panel, her eyes tracing the circuitry with an almost reverent focus. "This...this isn't standard," she murmured, more to herself than me.

"It's not," I confirmed. "The *Excalibur* has some...custom updates." I had been studying every aspect of the ship ever since I was condemned to play the part of Elias Thorne. The understatement was intentional, and the flicker in her eye told me she knew there was more to the story.

When we reached the officer's quarters, the disciplined ship order dissolved slightly. As we approached, a knot of young officers, their uniforms showing the patina of actual work rather than parade ground polish, snapped to attention.

From the variety of their comportment—

good-natured bantering, rapt debate, disgruntled complaining—they could have been any young men and women casually relaxing after a hard day's work, yet the subtle tension of their body language suggested they were concealing a shared disquiet.

"At ease," I said with a casual wave. "Dr. Haliday, may I introduce the finest team in the fleet? If you have any questions about anything, they're your people. Just don't believe everything they tell you about their last shore leave," I added, a smile on my lips. I was beginning to grow comfortable in my disguise as their captain.

"This our weapon's officer, John Steadman," I said, pointing to the short, chunky, sandy-haired man beside me. Then, I went around the room quickly, naming the men and women I had only recently met myself.

As the introductions followed, smiles and questions flew as fast as the respectful but undeniably curious glances they cast at Kate. Suddenly, I saw a glimpse of what the camaraderie of my crew could be like without the shadow of my deception. It made the lie feel all the more bitter.

Dinner in the wardroom was meant to be a formal affair, a reminder of hierarchy and order amidst the randomness of space. But this evening felt more like a gathering of excited scientists than a military function.

Commander Varek let his perfectly even white teeth sink into a succulent piece of sirloin steak. He chewed the morsel thoroughly before fixing his strangely penetrating blue eyes on me. For a moment our gaze met and exchanged a measure of our intense dislike.

The son of a rich and powerful shipping magnate, Varek had enjoyed a life of privilege, growing up poised and self-assured. Tall with a powerful physique, jet black hair, and cold blue eyes, he was strikingly handsome. When he chose to, he could display a dazzling smile.

I, on the other hand, had clawed my way up from the depths of poverty, fighting for every scrap of recognition and respect. The twist of fate that had landed me at this table felt like a cosmic joke, a reminder of the vast chasm that separated me from the likes of Varek.

Nevertheless, the dinner proceeded with some jovial bantering. My good-natured, loud, infectious laugh was frequently heard whenever someone ventured a quick joke.

"So, dark matter—is it as sticky as the textbooks imply?" This was from Lieutenant Chen, the ship's irrepressible astrogator, whose bright eyes gleamed with curiosity.

Kate launched into an explanation with the officers leaning forward. Their banter faded in favor of intense, focused conversation. Even Commander Varek seemed to forget his suspicion momentarily, his gaze fixed on Kate with begrudging respect.

"But what does it feel like?" asked Midshipman Angelica Nicole. She had an irrepressible bubbly personality. "I mean, if you could touch it."

I hid a smile. It was the kind of question only someone young and impossibly earnest would dare to pose. Kate, however, didn't bat an eye.

"It's not about touch, Angelica," she said. "It's about the taste." Then she lapsed into an almost hysterical laugh.

The sound of her laughter, so pure and unguarded, stirred something within me. For a fleeting instant, the weight of my deception seemed to lift, replaced by a sense of belonging I hadn't realized I craved.

As the evening drew close, I escorted Kate to the docking bay.

At the hanger hatch, Kate paused, her ever-watchful eyes holding mine for an unnervingly long moment. "Today was..." she began, then shook her head as if searching for the right word, "...unexpectedly joyous, Captain."

"We do try to keep our guests entertained," I returned, matching her smile.

"Thank you, Elias." The use of the first name, a subtle shift in formality, sent a ripple of warmth through me.

"You're welcome, Kate."

As the airlock opened, we stepped into the hangar bay.

A sense of hope flickered to life within me, a fragile counterpoint to the ever-present dread. The imposter and the brilliant scientist might yet forge a tentative peace. For now, that might be enough.

◆ ◆ ◆

The roar of the *Excalibur* faded into the distance as I expertly guided the small two-seater V-111 Firebird toward Newville with Kate sitting beside me. The thirty-minute trip stretched into something comfortable.

I said, "Fire retros, half power." The AI promptly reacted to cause the tiny craft to fall from its vertiginous orbit.

I loved flying the Firebird with its supercharged turbojet engine. It was a stratosphere, twin-seat utility craft designed to transport individuals and critical supplies between the ship and planets. Fast and durable but unarmed.

The tiny ship's port offered a bird's eye view of the planet. The fulsome imagery was a joy. I could appreciate its novelty as we plunged downward toward the broad terrain. The sunlight accentuated the blue skies, the vibrant blue-green oceans, and the orange-red horizon. These soon gave way to the planetary features of numerous rugged brown-gray mountains.

The craft penetrated the atmosphere and passed through the dotted white clouds with the moonlight reflecting off its polished surface. The hull creaked from strain, alerting me to the many and varied external noises—a startling change from the formal silence of deep space. Buffeted by winds and the air pressure, the ship's metal fabric made vibrating noises. Kate and I listened to a cacophony of thunderous rocket engines bellowing as fuel gurgled though the nozzles and then exploded out the exhaust.

Kate smiled when we started the final approach to the landing strip at the outer edge of the research facility.

"Impressive," she commented, watching my deft maneuvers with the controls. "I didn't realize you were a pilot on top of everything else."

A hint of a smile flickered across my lips. "It's a useful skill in my line of work. I picked it up some time ago," I said in a tone that discouraged further questions, for in truth, I had only rudimentary training and very few actual flights. I relied on AI to handle most of the maneuvering.

The gentle hum of the engines filled the space between us, a backdrop for a different kind of exploration.

Hesitantly, Kate ventured, "You never really talk about yourself, Elias. You seem so young to have achieved the rank of captain. What were you like... before all this?"

My grip on the control yoke tightened slightly, but I didn't deflect the question. Instead, I seemed to consider it carefully. "Complicated," I finally admitted, a wry touch to my voice. "Always restless, I suppose. I craved a bigger canvas than the one life seemed to offer."

"Sounds a bit familiar," Kate murmured, eyes tracing the constellations sparkling just beyond the shuttlecraft's viewport.

A comfortable silence settled between us, a silent understanding that some wounds were better left untouched for now. Then, as if a switch had flipped, I seemed to relax. A genuine warmth entered my gaze as I studied her. "Tell me about that treasure chest," I said quietly.

She blinked, the shift in conversation jarring in its unexpectedness. "Chest?"

"The one you talked about at dinner with your father's letters and family photos. The ghost of him, as you put it."

Kate looked away, out at the shimmering stars, instantly regretting sharing that personal information during the tour. "It's a strange thing, isn't it? To be defined by someone you hardly knew." Yet my question and the gentleness within it pulled the old memories forth.

"He was a romantic, my father. Dreamy love letters to my mother interspersed with theoretical physics and the grandeur of the universe. It painted this picture of a man far removed from the reality of my mother's quiet pragmatism. When they settled here to start the research facility a decade ago, they left me on Earth to finish my education. I came to Janus after my mother passed away and my father invited me to work on his research team. He died two years ago, and I continued with his work since then."

She hesitated, choosing her words carefully. "There was a photo too, you see, of my mother. She was a woman with a fearless glint in her eyes... she felt closer to me than my father ever did."

"The woman who craves the stars," I said, seeing much of Kate in her mother.

Kate nodded, a small smile playing on her lips. "I suppose I do. We all chase something, don't we? A ghost, a dream, a version of ourselves we long to become."

I shuddered. Those words were too close to the mark.

Silence settled again, but this time it felt companionable. The outline of the base gleamed ahead, a beacon pulling us back to reality.

"Thank you," I said, as I began landing procedures. My voice was low and sincere. "For sharing that."

CHAPTER 8

Verdict

Deep within the swirling nebula that cloaked their home world, the OV'aa council chamber pulsed with an eerie bioluminescence. The OV'aa were beings of intellect and shadow, who had mastered the art of weaving the fabric of dark and light matter into the tapestry of their existence.

The OV'aa thrived in a world unlike any other, where the veil between dark matter and ordinary matter was not just thin but interwoven. The planet pulsed with the harmonious dance of Eclipsion particles and atoms, a symphony of existence that the OV'aa had learned to conduct.

Their cities were marvels of this unique coexistence, floating islands in the void, held aloft by the subtle repulsions and attractions of Eclipsion particles. The buildings shimmered with a ghostly light constructed from materials that were both there and not.

The OV'aa themselves were a sight to behold,

forms that flickered at the edge of perception. They communicated not through sound but through ripples in the dark matter field, sending waves of thought and emotion that resonated in the hearts and minds of their kin.

But this harmony was not without its challenges. Their planets, for all their beauty, were a place of delicate balance. The Eclipsion particles, the very heart of their world, were capricious. Too much manipulation, and the islands could drift apart or collide. Too little, and the fabric of their reality could tear, exposing them to the raw chaos of unbridled forces.

Among the OV'aa, there were those known as the Weavers, gifted individuals who could manipulate the Eclipsion particles with unparalleled finesse. They were the caretakers, the guardians of the balance, ensuring that the dance of light and shadow never faltered.

Elder Xi'ara, her shimmering carapace etched with the wisdom of millennia, addressed the assembled advisors.

"The humans," she began, her voice resonating, "have progressed at an alarming rate. Even though our home star, Ophiuchi, is seventeen light years from Earth, it is less than five from Cygni."

A holographic display flickered to life. It depicted the human base nestled on Janus' surface. Another image showed a detailed schematic of the facility. It highlighted the churning heart of their operation – the dark matter reactor.

"Their rudimentary grasp of dark matter manipulation is...unexpected," conceded Councilor Nk'ala, his voice a rasping whisper.

"Intriguing, yes," Xi'ara agreed, "but a potential threat to our own energy exploitation. We cannot allow their reckless tinkering to destabilize the local dark matter flow and disrupt our harvesting efforts."

Councilor Xylia, a young OV'aa with bioluminescent markings that pulsed with agitation, spoke. "They are also establishing a rudimentary colony in the star system."

"A clear sign of territorial ambitions," Xi'ara stated, her voice hardening. "We cannot permit them to encroach further."

A tense silence descended upon the chamber. The humans were unpredictable, a savage yet ingenious species driven by a relentless quest for knowledge and expansion. Their presence in the Cygni system posed a significant risk.

"We cannot simply...eliminate them," Nk'ala ventured, the suggestion laced with unease. "The consequences for a public backlash would be severe."

"Indeed," Xi'ara replied, thoughtfully. "A more... subtle approach is required."

With a flick of her appendages, she activated another holographic projection. A sleek, multi-tentacled warship bristling with energy cannons. It dwarfed the crude human vessel at Janus by a factor of four.

"We will establish a permanent surveillance network around the Cygni system," she announced.

"A squadron of these cruisers will monitor human activity and provide early warning of transgressions."

A collective hum of approval resonated through the chamber.

"Furthermore," Xi'ara continued, a glint in her multifaceted eyes, "covert disruptions shall be implemented. Delays in resource shipments, 'accidents' at their facilities, a nudge here, a setback there..."

There was a satisfied chorus of clicks and hisses. The council relished manipulating the humans from the shadows. The subtly hindering of their progress without resorting to outright warfare was best.

Finally, Xi'ara unveiled the ultimate deterrent. Another holographic image materialized. It was a vast fleet of warships, their hulls radiating a cold, menacing light.

"This," she declared, her voice echoing with power, "is our battle fleet. It shall remain cloaked within the nebula, a silent guardian against human aggression. Should their actions escalate beyond acceptable bounds, this fleet will ensure their swift and complete eradication."

The chamber pulsed with a blinding luminescence as the council unanimously approved Xi'ara's plan. Humans posed a threat, but not an impossible one. The OV'aa, with their superior technology and millennia of experience, would ensure the safety of their dark matter harvesting operation. And they would maintain control of the Cygni system.

Yet, a seed of unease flickered within Xi'ara. Humans were an intriguing anomaly in the galactic tapestry. They could be troubling.

OV'aa would be watching and waiting.

CHAPTER 9

Chat

The Janus research lab hummed with its usual energy, a symphony of whirring machines and soft beeps punctuated by the occasional burst of excited chatter. Kate stood hunched over a monitoring console. Her brow furrowed was in concentration as she pored over the latest data readouts. The research into dark matter had opened a whole new realm of possibilities, and she was determined to unravel every last mystery.

"Hard at work as always, I see," a friendly voice called out, breaking Kate's focus.

She looked up to see Lieutenant Ayne Chalamet striding into the lab, a toolbox in one hand and a warm smile on her face. Kate couldn't help but return the smile. In the weeks since the dinner aboard the *Excalibur*, she and Ayne had grown close, bonding over their shared passion for their work and their mutual respect for a certain enigmatic captain.

"Ayne, I didn't expect to see you here today,"

Kate said, straightening up and stretching her back. "What brings you to my little corner of the universe?"

Ayne hefted the toolbox. "Just some routine calibration adjustments. Got to keep these babies," she slapped the console, "fine-tuned and happy."

She set to work, her deft fingers making alternations on the delicate sensors. As she worked, she cast a sideways glance at Kate. "So, how are things going with our illustrious Captain Thorne? I noticed you two have been spending quite a bit of time together lately."

Kate felt a flush creep up her neck. "Oh, you know," she said, trying to sound nonchalant. "Just comparing notes, discussing the mission. The usual."

Ayne arched an eyebrow. "Uh-huh. And I'm sure that's all there is to it."

Kate sighed, a smile tugging at the corners of her mouth. "Okay, fine. I'll admit it. He's...intriguing. Not at all what I expected from an SOS captain."

Ayne nodded, her expression turning thoughtful. "I know what you mean. When I first met him, I was prepared for some hardened, battle-scared veteran. But he's . . . different."

"Right," Kate said, leaning against the console. "He's so young, for one thing. I mean, how does someone that age end up commanding a ship like the *Excalibur*?"

"Talent, I guess. And charisma. He's got that in spades."

Kate chuckled. "No arguing there. When he walks into a room, it's like gravity shifts. Everyone's eyes just naturally turn to him."

Ayne grinned. "Doesn't hurt that he's easy on the eyes, too."

"Ayne!" Kate swatted at her friend's arm, but she couldn't suppress a giggle. "But yeah, I'll give you that. Those hazel eyes, that jawline...he's definitely not hard to look at."

"And the way he carries himself," Ayne added, her tone turning more serious. "There's confidence there, natural leadership. But it's not arrogance. He listens, he cares."

Kate nodded, her thoughts turning to the long conversations had shared with him, the way he always seemed genuinely interested in her work and her ideas. "He's not what I expected from the stories about the SOS. Those guys have a reputation for being...intense."

Ayne shrugged. "Maybe that's why he's a captain. He's got skills, but he's also got heart, not at all in keeping with the SOS reputation."

"Still," Kate said, a note of concern creeping into her voice, "it can't be easy, being in command. The weight of all that responsibility."

"He wears it well, though," Ayne pointed out. "I've never seen him falter, never seen him show a hint of doubt."

"I wonder if that's just a mask," Kate mused. "If deep down, he's just as unsure as the rest of us. Without his uniform, he's just a man."

Ayne furrowed her brow and gave Kate a look. "Without . . ."

Kate took a second and then turned beet red.

Ayne finished her adjustments and straightened up, wiping her hands on her pants. "Well, if anyone could get past that mask he wears, my money's on you."

Kate blinked, startled. "Me? What do you mean?"

Ayne tilted her head to the side and raised her brows. "Come on, Kate. I've seen the way he looks at you. The way you both look at each other. There's a connection there, something special."

Kate felt her heart skip a beat. She'd felt it too, that spark, that sense of understanding that went beyond mere colleagues or even friends. But to hear it said out loud...

"I don't know, Ayne," she said, a hint of wistfulness in her tone. "He's a captain. I'm a scientist. And we're in the middle of a mission that could change things big time. It's not exactly the best time for...complications."

Ayne's expression softened. "Kate, listen. We're out here, on the edge of the unknown, facing god knows what. If there's one thing I've learned, it's that you can't let fear or doubt hold you back. If you feel something, if you have a chance at happiness, you owe it to yourself to grab it with both hands. Besides if you're not interested, there may be others who might jump in."

"What?!" Kate exclaimed laughing. "Don't you dare."

Kate was silent for a long moment, letting

Ayne's words sink in. She thought of his strength, his compassion, the way he made her feel like anything was possible. And in that moment, she realized that her friend was right. In a universe filled with uncertainty, one thing was crystal clear: what she felt for this man was real, and it was worth fighting for.

"You know," she said at last, a slow smile spreading across her face, "you're pretty wise."

Ayne grinned. "I have my moments. Now, let's talk about strategy. If we're going to get you and Captain Tall, Dark, and Handsome together, we're going to need a plan."

Kate laughed, feeling a weight lift from her shoulders. With Ayne by her side, and the promise of something beautiful on the horizon, suddenly the vastness of space didn't seem quite so daunting.

And deep in her heart, a small, persistent voice whispered that maybe, just maybe, the key to unlocking the mysteries of the universe lay not in the stars, but in the depths of a pair of hazel eyes.

CHAPTER 10

Missing

An alarm still echoed throughout the Janus facility like the shriek of a wounded animal. It was a jarring contrast to the usual symphony of low hums and beeps. It was a sound I had been dreading, a new threat to the facade I'd painstakingly maintained.

Kate burst into the central hub, her face flushed with an intoxicating blend of panic and dread. "The phase inhibitor is gone," she spat out the words, her eyes fixed on me as if I were personally responsible for the catastrophe.

"Gone?" I echoed, trying to sound merely shocked rather than terrified. I glanced towards Varek, standing just behind Kate. His face was a mask of disciplined calm, but I sensed a cold calculation behind those steely eyes. If this wasn't a malfunction, the commander wasn't just a bystander; he was a prime suspect.

"Not just gone," Kate clarified, her voice gaining

a frantic edge. "It's not in the lab, not in storage... it's nowhere in the inventory!"

My pulse hammered a frantic rhythm against my temples. I could do the math. A missing component wasn't merely a delay for Kate's precious experiment; it was a giant blinking arrow pointing towards my incompetence...or worse, my deception.

My security team and I had rushed to the lab after Kate's urgent message. My head began to throb, and I wanted to rip open the package of pain pills in my pocket, but I couldn't.

"I need that inhibitor for the next sequence," she continued, pacing in tight circles like a caged animal. "Without it, the containment fields destabilize too fast. It's too damn risky to continue without it."

"Dr. Haliday," I began, struggling to project an air of command that was crumbling by the second, "calm down. We'll do a full sweep, double-check—"

"Double-check what exactly, Captain?" The words, laced with acid, came from Varek. The commander stepped forward, his presence suddenly dominating the scene. "As I understand, our authority extends to delivering an inventory of equipment, yes? That's been done. Dr. Haliday's operating experimental equipment seems well outside of our scope."

I noticed a flicker of something like satisfaction in Varek's usually impassive gaze for the first time.

"Regulations dictate—" I started, but the words felt hollow.

"Forget regulations!" Kate interjected, her voice cracking with frustration. "Physics isn't going to obey your protocols. Without that inhibitor, the project is stalled, maybe indefinitely. And it vanished on your watch, gentlemen."

"It's possible someone simply moved it—" I began.

"Or possible," Varek interrupted, his tone chillingly smooth, "someone doesn't want the good doctor to succeed. Perhaps afraid her work would expose...irregularities, let's say."

Every eye in the room was on me. The scientists, with their mix of confusion and thinly veiled disdain, the crewmen with a sense of wariness creeping into their usual loyalty. I could feel the fragile structure of authority slipping from my grasp like sand.

"We can't jump to conclusions," I insisted, but my attempt at strength felt feeble even to my ears.

The silence that followed was an accusation by itself.

I turned to Master Chief Kovalenko and barked, "Search the ship, the landing site, and the warehouses," The desperation in my voice sounded harsher than intended. "Turn over every crate, every locker in this laboratory and on *Excalibur*. No one leaves until we find that device." I forced myself to meet Varek's gaze. "That includes you, Commander."

It was a reckless gamble, but my options were rapidly dwindling. If the inhibitor wasn't found, my situation would be doomed.

And if it was, whoever took had their own agenda that I needed to discover.

The search began, a frantic tearing apart of the *Excalibur's* ordered compartments. I paced the corridors, every whispered conversation among my crew sounding like a condemnation. The minutes stretched into an agonizing eternity.

Then, like a fist clenching around my heart, there was a report from the lower engineering decks.

Kovalenko reported, "Captain... we've got something. You'll want to see this."

CHAPTER 11

In the Black

Life aboard the Excalibur fell into a tense, brittle rhythm after the debacle of the missing phase inhibitor. It had been found mysteriously mislabeled in a storage locker, but the incident left a lingering sense of unease. Kate eyed me with concern, her work resuming but now tinged with an undercurrent of resentment. Varek, ever watchful, seemed to lurk around every corner, his silence more foreboding than an open challenge.

I retreated to the solitude of my quarters, seeking solace in the familiar flicker of Thorne's logs on the stolen laptop. Thorne was a man of mystery and intrigue, haunted by shadows that I couldn't fully comprehend.

That night, a different kind of shadow found me.

I awoke with a jolt, my quarters bathed in the sickly green glow of an emergency alert. The familiar thrum of the ship was overlaid with a dissonant whine.

Once more an insistent pulsing headache pounded against my skull in sync with the whining.

Rushing to the bridge, I found the OOD, Lieutenant Ayne Chalamet, gesturing frantically towards a cluster of blinking lights. "Captain! Long-range scans are picking up energy fluctuations in Sector 48-Delta. Unexplained spikes, nothing consistent with known celestial objects, sir."

My heart sank. This couldn't be a coincidence, not after everything. Turning to Master Chief Kovalenko, I asked, "Readings?"

"Inconclusive, sir. Shifts in frequency, density... It's like something's out there, moving erratically, but the signals are too weak to get a clear picture." The chief continued, "I thought it was a malfunction at first, but now..."

"Now what?" I pressed.

Kovalenko swallowed hard. "We're getting similar readings on multiple instruments, Captain. It's something."

I slowed my breathing, trying to quell the rising panic in my gut. Real emergencies on top of manufactured ones? Neither of which offered any clarity.

I glanced around, desperately seeking Varek's presence, but that ever-present ghost was nowhere to be found. I was alone in this.

"Magnify the sector. Record everything," I ordered, my voice steadier than I felt. "Tell me everything you can about those fluctuations."

Hours turned into an eternity spent staring at distorted images and snippets of data that made little sense. The chief's initial apprehension had given way to a morbid fascination. He rattled off theoretical possibilities—rogue asteroids, unknown pulsar phenomena, even the far-fetched notion of a drifting nebula. Each explanation seemed more inadequate than the last.

When the alert finally subsided, I collapsed onto my bunk. Sleep was impossible. My head throbbed and my mind spiraled into terrifying conjecture.

Is this connected to the Janus project somehow?

Or was it a symptom of my fraying sanity, the ghosts of my deception whispering madness into the silence of deep space?

I shut my eyes tight, trying to will the chaos of my thoughts into submission. But the rhythmic thump of my headache continued. It throbbed in time with the hum of the ship. It was a mocking reminder that the darkness held secrets I couldn't comprehend. I reached for the pain pills, but my fingers found Thorne's laptop.

I scanned the familiar text which offered no answers, only the haunting question from one of the final log entries: "Is something out there. She knows. Must contact."

What does that mean?

My gaze drifted out of the viewport to space's uncaring blackness.

CHAPTER 12

Chatter

The mess hall of the Excalibur was a hive of activity, the clatter of dishes and the hum of conversation filling the air. In a corner, huddled around a table laden with steaming mugs and an assortment of snacks, sat a group of the ship's key personnel.

As they sipped their coffee, the conversation turned to the latest gossip.

Lieutenant Horatio Chen leaned back in his chair, cradling his mug. "Another day, another stretch of uncharted space," he mused. "You know, when I signed up to navigate this mission, I thought I'd at least know more about where we were heading."

Data security officer Lieutenant Stamos nodded; his brow furrowed. "It's all a bit hush-hush, isn't it? I mean, I get the need for secrecy, but it'd be nice to have some idea of what we're getting into."

"That's the SOS for you," weapons officer John Steadman chimed in. "Always playing things close to the vest."

Master Chief Kovalenko snorted. "Close to the vest? More like locked up tighter than a Martian bank vault. I've been in this fleet for over two decades, and I still don't know half of what those spooks get up to."

"What about our new captain?" Midshipman Angelica Nicole asked, her young face a mix of curiosity and apprehension. "Anyone know anything about him?"

A moment of silence descended on the group. They exchanged glances, each searching their memory for any scrap of information about me, the enigmatic Elias Thorne.

"Not much," Chen admitted at last. "Just the usual rumors and scuttlebutt. They say he's some kind of prodigy, rose through the ranks faster than anyone in history."

Stamos leaned forward, lowering his voice conspiratorially. "I heard he once took down a whole pirate fleet with just a single ship. Supposedly, he's got tactics and maneuvers that are out of this world."

Steadman shook his head. "I don't buy it. No one's that good, not even an SOS hotshot. There's got to be more to the story."

Kovalenko stroked his chin thoughtfully. "You know, now that you mention it, I do remember hearing something a while back. Something about a mission that went sideways, a whole squad lost. Thorne was the only survivor."

Nicole's eyes widened. "You think that's why he's so...intense? Because of what happened to his team?"

"Could be," Kovalenko said with a shrug. "Trauma like that, it changes a person. Makes them harder, more driven."

"But why put him in charge of this mission?" Chen wondered aloud. "I mean, if he's such a loose cannon..."

"Maybe that's exactly why," Stamos suggested. "Maybe they need someone who's not afraid to take risks or to push the boundaries."

Steadman leaned back, crossing his arms over his chest. "Well, I just hope he knows what he's doing. We're a long way from home. If something goes wrong... I'm only saying . . ."

"Hey," Nicole said, a note of optimism in her voice. "We're the crew of the Excalibur. We can face tough times and come out on top. Whatever Captain Thorne has in store for us, we'll handle it."

Kovalenko chuckled, reaching over to ruffle Nicole's hair. "Listen to the pup, all full of hope and bravado. Reminds me of myself, back in the day."

The tension in the room eased a bit as laughter rippled around the table.

"All right, then," Chen said, raising his mug. "To the *Excalibur*, and to whatever the hell we're doing out here. May the stars guide us, and the engines keep running."

"And may the captain know his ass from a black hole," Steadman added with a grin.

They clinked their mugs together. And whatever secrets they thought Captain Elias Thorne, might be hiding, they knew one thing for certain: the crew of the *Excalibur* would face it head-on.

CHAPTER 13

Breakthrough

The Janus research lab was a pressure cooker of tension, the air thick with the lingering mistrust born from the missing inhibitor incident. Kate moved through this minefield with a careful tread. Her once-fiery determination was now tempered by the weight of doubt. The gleaming equipment that surrounded her now seemed to mock her with its cold, distorted reflections.

I addressed the research team.

"Dr. Haliday," I began, "perhaps you and your colleagues should consider a small-scale test, before risking another major effort."

Kate's eyes flashed. "Risks are inherent in progress, Captain. Or had you forgotten?"

Under the intensity of her gaze, the respect we had once shared was now suspect.

I said, "Very well, Dr. Haliday. You can proceed with your outline major test."

"Thank you, Captain."

Finally able to take the plunge, Kate was eager to get started. The team scrambled to bring all the equipment online. They ran through an extensive calibration process. The checklist was scanned, and each step was meticulously completed.

Dr. Austin Harrison said, "Laser power set to test level. Ready to commence energy pulse."

Kate took a deep breath. "Initiate."

Harrison pressed the button, and the laser shot a pulse into space.

Kate read the sensor readings reacting to the interference patterns appearing in space where the laser struck.

After all their painstaking effort, that afternoon they achieved a breakthrough.

It crept in on silent feet, a data anomaly so minuscule it nearly escaped notice.

"It's happening!" Harrison, his earnest eyes peering out from beneath a mop of unruly hair, was the first to spot it. With a trembling finger, he pointed to a blip on his screen, a tiny spike in the otherwise flat landscape of data.

Harrison was a man who's very being was entangled with the stars. Born to renowned astrophysicists, he had been steeped in the language of the cosmos from his earliest days. Yet, for all his theoretical knowledge, it was the tangible, the hands-on application of discovery, that truly set his soul alight.

"I think..." he began, his voice a tentative whisper. Then, as if finding strength in the data before him, his words gained conviction. "...I think we just destabilized a cluster of dark matter particles for a fraction of a second."

To Kate, those words were a thunderclap, a seismic shift. She went utterly still, her breath caught in her throat, as if the slightest movement might shatter this fragile moment. Then, in a burst of energy, she was at Harrison's side, her eyes devouring the screen.

The hours that followed were a blur of frenzied activity to confirm the finding. The lab became a self-contained universe.

When the final data fell into place, Kate slumped back in her chair. The adrenaline that had sustained her drained away. In that moment of utter exhaustion, she seemed diminished. When she finally spoke, her voice was a tremulous whisper.

"We did it," she breathed, wonder and disbelief intertwined in each syllable. "We produced controlled energy from dark matter."

For Kate, it was the realization of a dream that had consumed her.

CHAPTER 14

Connecting

In the days following the dark matter breakthrough, I was drawn to the Janus research lab as a silent observer amidst the buzzing activity. I watched as Kate and her team pored over the data unaffected by their mix of exhaustion and exhilaration.

In these quiet moments, stolen between the demands of my duties, I began to see more of Kate. I marveled at her dedication and how she threw herself into her work with passion. It was a quality I recognized in myself, a driving need to prove my worth, to make a difference.

One evening, as the lab emptied, I found Kate hunched over her workstation, her eyes heavy with fatigue.

"Kate," I said softly.

"Kate," I repeated.

She looked up, blinking as if emerging from a dream. "I didn't hear you come in."

I smiled. "I think it's time you called it a night. Even brilliant scientists need their rest."

Kate chuckled, a sound that seemed to surprise even herself. "Is that an order, Captain?"

"More like a friendly suggestion. Your work will still be here in the morning."

She hesitated, glancing back at the screens. "I suppose you're right. It's just... there's so much to do and understand."

I nodded, moving to lean against the workstation beside her. "I know the feeling. The weight of responsibility coupled with the fear of letting people down."

Kate looked at me then, really looked at me. I felt a flicker of understanding pass between us.

"How do you do it?" she asked. "How do you shoulder your burden?"

I was silent for a long moment, considering my words. "By remembering that I'm not alone," I said at last. "I have a crew who support me and will save me if I fall."

"And do you? Fall, I mean?"

"More often than I'd like to admit," I said with a rueful smile. "But that's the thing about leadership and about pushing boundaries. Sometimes, you stumble, pick yourself up, and keep going."

Kate's gaze drifted back to the endless scroll of data. "I've spent my whole life chasing this," she murmured. "This dream of unlocking the secrets of the universe. And now that we're on the cusp of something incredible, I can't help but wonder...

what happens next? What happens when the dream becomes reality?"

I placed my hand on her shoulder. "You keep dreaming," I said softly. "You find a new horizon to chase, a new mystery to unravel. That's the beauty of science. And of space exploration, for that matter. There's always something more to discover."

Kate looked at me, her eyes bright. "Thank you," she whispered. "For understanding."

In that moment, I felt a surge of emotion, a connection that ran deep. In the quiet of the lab, we were simply two people, each grappling with the weight of our fears.

"What do you do to relax? Where you're not driving yourself with work?" I asked.

"Well, I love to sail. The open ocean is my freedom to truly escape from the lab."

"Sounds wonderful," I said.

"Would like to go sailing? A chance to experience a different environment from space?"

"I'd like that. Whenever you can find the time."

Over the next few days, Kate and I gravitated toward each other, stealing moments of quiet conversation amidst the mission's chaos. We talked of our pasts, hopes, and fears, each revealing a tiny crack in the walls we had built around ourselves.

For Kate, I became a sounding board for the doubts and insecurities that plagued her. She spoke of the pressure to live up to her father's legacy, the fear of failure that haunted her. In me, she found a kindred spirit, someone who understood the toll of wearing a mask, of pretending to be more than you were.

And for me, Kate became a reminder of what I was fighting for, of the dreams and aspirations that drove me forward. In her passion, I saw a reflection of my hunger to leave a mark.

It was a fragile bond. But for now, that was enough.

CHAPTER 15

Tea

As work in the science lab continued, crews constructed new more advanced experimental equipment. The once pristine base was now strewn with miscellaneous gear and machines hastily positioned. Kate was confined to analysis of experimental data and writing reports.

Varek's animosity towards me hung between us like a storm cloud, an uncomfortable echo of his accusations buzzing in her ears. She saw his veiled suspicion in every glance, his disapproval every time I checked in on her progress. It left her disquieted.

As Kate poured over the data logs, she searched for ways to further the results. Nothing in the readings hinted at instability or an impending problem.

My visits were the highlight of her now restricted existence. I spoke little about my interactions with Varek, but the tension in my shoulders and the perpetually grim set of my mouth were telling.

As the double suns descended one evening, Harrison said, "We have a situation."

"What?" Kate asked, bracing herself.

"Possibly signs of something . . .? Power surges throughout the base. Systems are failing. Nothing we do seems to isolate the problem."

"Sabotage?" She voiced the chilling possibility.

Harrison nodded. "It looks that way. The question is, who and how are they doing it?"

The investigation that followed was maddening. Every circuit traced, every piece of tech examined... and nothing. The base flickered in and out of darkness, communications faltered. It was as if some unseen force was toying with them.

Then, it hit her. It was so simple, so terrifying in its implications that she gasped aloud.

"What is it?" Harrison was at her side in an instant.

"The power fluctuations... they're not random. They have a pattern."

Within the hour, Kate's theory was confirmed. An unknown technology was interfering with their gear over vast distances. It was insidious. And the implications were potentially devastating.

The power fluctuations at the Janus research facility concerned me. The mystery of their origin gnawed at me. I knew that the stability of the station's energy grid was crucial to the success of the dark matter experiments, and any disruption could have catastrophic consequences.

I stood on the bridge of the *Excalibur*; my brow furrowed as I studied the latest reports from the station. The readings were erratic, the spikes and dips in power levels defying any logical explanation. It was as if some unseen force was toying with us.

I turned to Varek and gestured to the data on the screen. I said, "Something is going on, and I'm going to get to the bottom of it."

Varek raised an eyebrow. "With all due respect, Captain, we have more pressing matters to attend to. The *Excalibur's* maintenance procedures are still ongoing."

I shook my head, my jaw set with determination. "No, this takes priority. If we lose power on Janus, we lose the station."

For a moment, Varek looked as if he might argue. His hostility towards me was a simmering resentment. But as he studied the data on the screen, even he had to concede the point. The power fluctuations were a threat that could not be ignored.

"Very well," he said at last, grudgingly. "What do you propose?"

I considered for a moment, my mind racing with possibilities. "I need answers," I said. "And I think I know where to start looking."

I turned to leave the bridge, pausing at the threshold. "I think I'll get some tea," I said, a hint of a smile playing at the corners of my mouth.

Varek blinked, confused by the sudden shift in topic. But before he could respond, I was gone, my footsteps echoing down the corridor.

A few hours later I returned to the bridge of *Excalibur*.

"Helm, set course for the asteroid belt," I ordered.

When we reached my designated coordinates, I turned the conn over to the OOD and went to the hanger bay.

My eyes fixed on the small, agile craft that rested on the launch pad.

As I climbed into the cockpit of the Firebird, I felt a thrill. With a roar of its engines, the Firebird lifted off from the hangar bay, streaking out into space. I pushed the throttle forward, feeling the G-forces press me back into my seat as the craft accelerated.

My destination was Raja, a small but infamous outpost nestled deep within the asteroid belt. I landed on the outskirts and began walking into the rusty town.

The dimly lit streets of the notorious asteroid colony nestled deep within the Cygni star system seemed to pulse with a life of their own. Once a thriving mining community, the depletion of its mineral riches had left behind a husk of a settlement, a labyrinth of abandoned structures and rusting infrastructure. In the vacuum left by the exodus of honest workers, a new breed of inhabitants had taken root—the desperate, the cunning, and the dangerous.

I navigated the narrow, twisting alleyways with a sense of purpose, my disguise carefully crafted to blend in with the colony's eclectic mix of residents. My hair now unkempt strands of dyed inky black. Expertly applied makeup gave my skin a shallow, unhealthy pallor. The final touch, a set of yellowed, misshapen false teeth, completed the illusion of a man who had spent far too long on the fringes of society.

As I approached the entrance to a seedy bar, a flickering neon sign cast an eerie glow.

Somewhere within this den of thieves and cutthroats lay the key to unraveling a mystery that had haunted the Earth Imperium for months —whispers of shadowy figures seeking information about the groundbreaking research being conducted on Janus.

The very reason why an SOS officer was sent to Cygni!

I stepped through the bar's threshold. The interior was anarchy. Patrons huddled around small tables; their faces obscured by the haze of smoke. Shouting and threats that could lead to violence at any moment.

Making my way to an empty table near the back of the room, I settled into a chair. I scanned the crowd, my eyes searching for the contact who had promised me information.

I couldn't shake the feeling that I was being watched.

A waiter came by. I ordered, "Yellow chamomile tea, please."

The waiter nodded and disappeared.

Time ticked by until an hour had passed. Just as I was beginning to wonder if I had wasted my time, a figure slid into the seat across from me. The man was older, his face lined and weathered, but his eyes gleamed with a sharp intelligence that belied his unassuming appearance.

"You must be Thorne," the man said, his voice low and gruff. "I'm Wyden."

I nodded. "I was told that you had information about Raja."

Wyden leaned forward, his elbows resting on the table's scarred surface. "Not just Raja," he corrected. "They've been making inroads throughout the Cygni system, even as far as Janus."

"Who?"

"I don't know exactly. I've never seen them or met anyone who has seen them. But I've heard all the stories."

"What stories?"

"That there are some weird strangers who skulk about offering big money for basic information. They are heavily covered in strange clothes, and everyone has a different description of them. But they all want information and are willing to pay in raw gems."

"What do they want?" I asked, my mind racing with possibilities.

Wyden shook his head. "That's the million-credit question, isn't it? Some say they're after technology, others think they're scouting for an invasion. But there are whispers..." He trailed off, his gaze darting around the room as if to ensure we weren't being overheard.

"Whispers of what?"

"That they're searching for something specific. Something related to the experiments on Janus."

I felt a surge of adrenaline course through my veins.

"How do you know all this?" I asked, my eyes narrowing in suspicion.

Wyden smiled. "In a place like Raja, information is the most valuable currency. I've spent years cultivating contacts, building a network that spans every level. When these very strange 'strangers' started making inquiries, I was one of the first to hear about it."

I leaned back in my chair, my mind whirling with the implications of Wyden's revelations. If these stranger 'strangers' were aliens and they contacted the gangs that controlled Raja's underworld, the situation would be even more dire than I had feared. The gangs were notoriously unpredictable, their loyalties shifting with the winds of profit and power. If they had allied themselves with aliens...

"I need proof," I said at last, my voice firm. "I can't take this to my superiors without concrete evidence."

Wyden reached into his coat, withdrawing a

small data chip. He held it up, the bar's dim light glinting off its polished surface. "Everything I know and have been able to gather is on this chip," he said. "Recordings of conversations, surveillance footage, even a few supposed photos of the 'strangers' themselves."

I reached for the chip, but Wyden pulled it back, a sly grin spreading across his face. "Not so fast," he admonished. "Information like this doesn't come cheap."

I sighed, reaching into my pocket, and withdrew a small bag. I opened it and spilled a few cut gems onto the table. I watched Wyden snatch them and inspect them. Satisfied, the older man slid the data chip across the table, where I pocketed it with relief.

"A pleasure doing business with you," Wyden said, his tone almost mocking. "But I'd watch my back if I were you. Others might be interested in what you're carrying."

With that cryptic warning, Wyden rose from his seat and melted into the crowd, leaving me alone. I knew I needed to get the data chip back to my ship to analyze its contents and plan my next move. But as I made my way towards the exit, I couldn't shake the feeling of walking into a trap.

As I stepped out into the alleyway, the door to the bar slamming shut behind me, I found myself face-to-face with a group of heavily armed men. They wore the colors of one of Raja's most notorious gangs. Their faces were twisted into sneers of cruel anticipation.

"Well, well, well," the leader drawled, his voice dripping with menace. "What do we have here? A little rat scurrying from where he doesn't belong?"

My hand drifted towards the concealed weapon at my waist, but I knew I was outnumbered and outgunned.

"I don't want any trouble," I said, my voice steady despite my heart pounding. "I'm just passing through."

The gang leader laughed, a harsh, grating sound. "Passing through, are you? With a pocketful of treasures?"

My blood ran cold. How could they know? Unless...

"Wyden," I whispered, realization dawning. The older man had sold me out.

"We want what you have," the gang leader continued, taking a step forward.

My mind raced, desperate for a way out. I knew I couldn't let the data chip fall into the wrong hands.

Just as I pulled out my gun, a shout rang out from the other end of the alleyway. A figure emerged from the shadows, his face obscured by a hood and a scarf. In his hand, he held a heavy blaster, its muzzle trained on the gang leader.

"Back off," the newcomer growled, his voice low and menacing. "He comes with me."

The gang leader hesitated, his eyes darting between me and the hooded figure. For a moment, it seemed as if he might back down. But then, with a roar of fury, he lunged forward, his weapon drawn.

Chaos erupted in the alleyway, blaster fire filling the air as the two sides exchanged shots. I dove for cover, my weapon in hand. I returned fire as best I could. The gang members fell one by one, their bodies crumpling to the ground in a haze of smoke and blood.

When the shooting finally stopped, I cautiously emerged from my hiding place, eyes scanning the alleyway for any movement. The hooded figure was still standing, his blaster trained on the last remaining gang member.

"Who are you?" I demanded. I had my weapon at the ready.

The figure reached up and pushed back his hood, revealing Kovalenko's haggard face.

"What are you doing here?" I asked with surprise.

Kovalenko grinned, holstering his blaster. "You didn't think I'd let you walk into this nest of vipers alone, did you? I've been tracking you since you left the ship."

I shook my head, a smile tugging at the corners of my mouth.

I like the Master Chief.

CHAPTER 16

Spirit

As I entered the marina, my eyes were immediately drawn to Kate. She stood at the end of a pier. Her gaze was lost looking at the sea. She looked radiant in a white halter and blue shorts, her hair pulled back in a ponytail with a yellow ribbon dancing in the breeze. For a moment, I simply stood there, content to admire her silhouette against the backdrop of the aquamarine waves.

A warm gust of wind broke my reverie.

"Kate?" I called.

Startled, she turned, and her eyes brightened with delight.

"Elias!"

"Apologies for coming up behind you," I said. "I was simply enchanted by the view."

"The ocean is beautiful today, isn't it?" she said, turning back to the horizon.

"I wasn't talking about the ocean," I replied.

"Thank you." Kate ducked her head, a faint

blush coloring her cheeks. "Now, are you ready to set sail, or do you plan to stand there staring all day?"

"Aye aye, Captain Haliday!" I saluted. My eyes twinkling as an incoming wave shattered against the nearby rocks, spraying us.

Kate's ten-meter yawl, the Spirit, was at the end of the pier. We climbed aboard.

Kate unfurled the jib sail while I hauled in the lines. The jib caught the wind, and we headed out.

She heaved on the helm to point the bow toward open water and pulled the sheets taut, letting the boat heel over. Kate's laughter rang out across the water, mingling with the cry of a sea bird overhead. The Spirit caught the wind and headed out to sea.

I couldn't help but marvel at the carefree joy on Kate's face.

Out here, away from the pressures of her lab and my mission, we seemed transformed. It was as if the salty air and the endless blue of the ocean had washed away both of our worries. We each looked forward to a well-deserved respite, a chance to recharge our lives.

We skirted a sandbar and passed the shore cliffs. Waves battered the jagged rocks that ringed the shore, sending up towers of spray.

"It's beautiful, isn't it?" Kate said, her voice almost reverent. "Sometimes, out here, it's easy to forget about everything else, all the challenges and uncertainties."

I nodded, understanding the sentiment all too well. "It's a different world, a chance to celebrate your victory. Out here the only thing that matters is the wind in the sails and the person beside you."

Kate met my gaze, her eyes soft and filled with an emotion I couldn't quite name. For a moment, the world fell away, leaving only the two of us.

As the Spirit sailed on, we fell into a comfortable rhythm, adjusting the sails and navigating the currents. We shared stories and jokes, our laughter carried away in the breeze.

Kate guided the boat with a sure hand, navigating through the choppy waters with practiced ease. The blustery summer breeze whipped around us, its salty tang invigorating our senses. The boat pitched and rolled in perfect harmony with the sea.

I admired her as she stood by the mast, her ponytail acting as a telltale.

"Kate," I yelled over the gusty weather.

She smiled, and balancing herself against the undulation of the deck, made her way to the cockpit. She sat sideways to me—her knees tucked under her, a happy smile on her face.

Seeing her zeal for adventure, I pulled her close.

"You love it, don't you?" I asked, snuggling against her. "Sailing."

"It's grand—sometimes tranquil, but always exhilarating."

We sailed for an hour until Kate led us to a tiny, deserted island with white beaches and a secluded cove.

I loosened the sails and let the waves carry the Spirit toward the shore. Kate dropped the anchor on the sandy bottom. Quickly furling the sails, I jumped over the side and turned to lift Kate off. I carried her through the rolling surf, thrilling to the feel of her arms around my neck. She didn't protest at all when I kissed her. Her lips pressed back with equal intent.

I returned to the boat for our picnic basket.

She spread a blanket out on the sand while I opened the basket. I laid out a tempting lunch, but we ate little, too engrossed in each other.

I asked, "How about a swim?"

"I didn't bring a bathing suit."

"That's not a problem."

I stood up and stripped. Then I ran head long into the water making a great splash and swam strongly out into the deeper water.

The act caught Kate completely by surprise.

She sat stunned for a moment, taken aback by my bold act. But as the initial shock wore off, a spark of excitement ignited within her. With an eager grin and a racing heart, she quickly shed her own clothes and dove into the water, ready to join me in spontaneous adventure.

In tandem we swam parallel to the beach for a mile and then doubled back.

When we came out of the water, our naked bodies glistened, but we were unabashed as we flopped down on the blanket, exhilarated and exhausted.

We watched as the incoming tide washed away our footprints. A flurry of spray splattered over us.

Kate lay back on the blanket, comfortable with

her nudity. When I moved beside her, she rolled closer —her lips moist and parted. She kissed me. I wrapped my arms around her and let our passion blossom.

Afterward, we lay together, content for a long time.

In the aftermath of our passion, I gazed out at the sunbaked sand and the glimmering blue water. I felt a sense of peace settle deep within me. In this precious moment, all the worries and responsibilities that weighed upon me seemed to melt away, carried off by the gentle sea breeze.

"Are you cold?" I asked.

"No." She snuggled comfortably into my arms. "I love you," she whispered.

The words sounded right.

"I love you too."

Before long, I sat up to scan the sky and asked, "Home now?"

"Just a little longer. The afternoon is grand. I want to make it last as long as possible."

I blinked. As I brushed a stray grain of sand from her cheek, I noticed the wind had begun to pick up, whipping the waves into frothy peaks. Reluctantly, I turned to Kate.

"As much as I hate to say it, we should probably head back. The wind's picking up."

Kate nodded. We dressed and packed up our gear. Together we got the yawl out of the surf and made our way back to sea.

The sun set as we docked.

CHAPTER 17

Anomalies

Aboard the Excalibur, the bridge hummed with tension transcending the usual battle readiness. Each flicker on the sensor panels sent ripples of unease through the crew. The sabotage on Janus had left them on edge.

I stood at the main viewport as my ship patrolled the Cygni system. The familiar tapestry of stars and nebulae felt alien now.

"Anything?" My voice was directed toward Lieutenant Chalamet, manning the sensor station.

"Just… fluctuations, sir," she replied, her voice strained. "Subtle distortions, almost like a mirage. Nothing consistent enough to identify as a ship."

I grimaced. This was the third such anomaly we'd detected in the past week.

Ghostly flickers on the edge of perception, hinting at a presence that remained stubbornly out of reach. Were these merely natural phenomena, or was it an alien cloaked in their insidious technology? I was certain this was confirmation of the information I had acquired from Raja.

"Chief Kovalenko, are those new sensor arrays ready?" I asked, turning towards the stern-faced Master Chief.

Kovalenko nodded curtly. "Aye, Captain. We've been running calibration checks non-stop. But the tech's...unconventional."

The word hung in the air, heavy with unspoken uncertainty. Kate's team of scientists had worked tirelessly for the past week to improve the sensor systems to deal with these persistent abnormalities. The new devices pushed boundaries, but this felt different—desperate times call for desperate measures.

A few days earlier, I had found Kate in one of the repurposed cargo bays, surrounded by a tangle of wires.

"Elias." She looked up, a flicker of surprise crossing her face. "I wasn't expecting you down here."

I hesitated, momentarily forgetting the urgency of my mission. "We need you, Kate. We need your..." I searched for a delicate way to phrase it, "...unconventional expertise."

A wry smile touched her lips. "So now I'm an asset, not a liability?"

"Kate, I...." My words failed me. "These anomalies we're finding as we patrol the planets, they could be ships, but our sensors..."

She nodded, cutting me off. "I know. I was suspicious of the interference we were having in the facility as well. The distortions are too subtle and interwoven with the space fabric itself. It's brilliant camouflage if that's what it is."

"So can you ..."

"We can try," she finished, her voice determined. We need to find a way to strip away the background noise, to see the signal through the distortion."

The next few days were a whirlwind of focused frenzy. I marshaled the ship's resources for Kate's testing, pushing the Excalibur's engineering capabilities to the limit. She worked with a single-minded intensity that left even the tireless Kovalenko breathless.

Her results came in quiet triumph rather than a dramatic explosion.

"I think...I think I have it," she said, staring at a screen filled with pulsing waveforms. "See the pattern here? It's faint, but it's there. A resonance, subtly out of phase with the natural fluctuations of subspace."

"Can you isolate it, enhance it?" I asked, my pulse quickening with anticipation and fear.

"With time, yes," Kate nodded, her usual confidence returning. "We'll need to build filters, amplifiers... It won't be perfect, but it might be enough to reveal what's out there."

In the dim light of the makeshift lab, a flicker of a smile crossed her lips. "Just a little more tinkering, and we might finally get a proper look at our ghosts."

Soon Kate's theoretical brilliance morphed into functioning detection prototypes.

I hastily rigged interfaces across Excalibur's sensor array. Lieutenant Chalamet's station now resembled a mad scientist's fever dream. Blinking lights, flickering waveforms, and an insistent hum thrummed through the ship.

On the bridge, I felt like a caged animal.

Kovalenko hovered near, his usual stoicism threaded with a nervous energy. The waiting was agony.

"Lieutenant," I barked. "Anything?"

Chalamet peered intently at the screen, her brow furrowed in concentration. "The distortions are still there, sir," she replied, her voice tight. "Stronger this time... but masked."

"Apply the upgraded filters," I ordered.

With a series of deft keystrokes, she activated Kate's sensor algorithms. The waveforms on the screen stuttered, then merged into something... sharper. This was no anomaly, no trick of light or stellar debris.

A stark image emerged. Sleek, elongated, and utterly alien.

Kovalenko gasped, "By all the saints..."

"Multiple contacts," Chalamet's voice was barely a whisper. "Several ships in a dispersed formation.

They're..." she paused, as if searching for the right words, "...observing us."

I ordered, "Helm, left full rudder, bring us to an intercept course with the lead ship."

"Aye aye, sir."

As the Excalibur maneuvered, the lead alien vessel pivoted on the main viewscreen, revealing a cluster of pulsating energy nodes—weapons— instinct screamed at me. But before I could utter a command, the alien ships turned and fled at high acceleration.

"They know," Kovalenko breathed, echoing the chill realization that settled over the bridge. "They know we saw them."

I turned to Chalamet. "Any residual readings? Anything we can use to track them?"

She shook her head, a flicker of despair in her eyes. "They're clean, sir. It's like they were never there."

"Except we know they were," I muttered.

We were no longer dealing with mere suspicion but a grim reality.

CHAPTER 18

Send Help

The *Excalibur's* bridge was tense as I stood at the central command console. My gaze swept over the projections of the holographic star map. Beside me, Chalamet was hunched over her station, scanning the interface as she fine-tuned the sensor array.

"We're approaching optimal scanning range," she announced. There was a nervous edge to her voice. "Activating now."

A ripple passed through the display. Previously barren sectors of the planet's orbit bloomed with readings—unmistakably alien energy signatures. One...no, two large vessels, previously cloaked, were now starkly visible against the backdrop of space.

"There they are," I breathed. The confirmation was disturbing. This was no longer a hunt for elusive enemies but a confrontation with a formidable force.

For a crucial, doubtful moment, nothing changed on the display. Then, the readings shifted.

"They know!" Chalamet gasped. "They've detected our scans!"

The alien vessels powered up. Weapon systems flickered to life across the gargantuan hulls.

I cursed. The alien vessels loomed on the viewscreen, their hulls pulsing with an eerie, otherworldly light. The sheer size of the ships dwarfed the Excalibur, making it seem like a mere speck in the vastness of space. As the crew watched in fascination and horror, the alien ships began to move, their movements fluid.

The enemy has launched missiles, sir," reported the sensor operator.

"Sound battle stations. Full power to the shields," I said calmly.

"They've fired lasers at extreme range," reported the weapons officer.

"Shields are holding," said Kovalenko.

Seconds ticked by as the missiles approached.

"Incoming missiles!" reported the sensor operator. "Range closing."

"Ahead full, left full rudder. Release sensor jammers and decoys." My voice was calm and steady, and no hint of doubt or worry showed.

A moment later, I said, "Fire anti-missile missiles."

The crew watched as the interception was successful, and the enemy missiles exploded harmlessly.

Steadman said, "They have an energy signature twice that of the Excalibur and are bristling with long-range weapons. I think they might be battlecruisers, maybe four times our strength. That would put the odds 8:1 against us."

"I don't believe in odds," I said. "I only believe in what I must do."

I took a deep breath. I was entirely at ease. Unlike my fear of being unmasked, which troubled me daily, I was unconcerned about combat. In my mind, getting caught as a fraud had consequences for me and my family, but being killed in combat meant an end to all my trouble.

I felt a thrill at the prospect of deadly combat. I had always relished physical challenges, and warfare was the ultimate personal test.

That's how I feel.

It was as if I had finally found my true calling in life.

All around me observed my relaxed demeanor and a hint of a smile.

Chalamet muttered, "He is relishing this."

And I was.

I spent a moment recalling Thorne's weapon tactics from the recovered log. I methodically considered each in my mind. I reviewed the types of battle maneuvers that would be most suitable in this circumstance.

The bridge crew awaited orders.

Finally, my mind was sharp and clear. I knew what I must do.

In rapid succession, I issued the orders, "Helm, hard to starboard. Ahead flank. I want to close the distance rapidly and bring maximum weapons to bear."

I turned to the weapon's officer, John Steadman, and said, "I want you to input an AI program to coordinate our weapons attack according to the following parameters:

- Fire full plasma blasters are at the lead ship at the optimal range. Use a broad dispersed pattern to blanket their sensor field.
- Launch a full missile spread and fire rail guns at the lead ship's weapon array. Time the launched missiles to arrive 1 second after the plasma bursts. The plasma speed is .7c, and the missile speed is .3c, so calculate carefully.
- Fire a laser barrage to hit the lead ship just as the missiles reach it."

I continued, "Once the barrage hits the target, perform the same tactic on the second ship. I will maneuver the Excalibur for defensive purposes, so be aware of our changing relative position as you fire."

Steadman said, "I've never heard of such . . ."

"You have your orders."

"Aye aye, sir. It will take me a few minutes to . . ."

"You have one minute, Mister Steadman. Get going."

Steadman snapped to it, and in one minute, he said, "Ready to fire on the first ship as ordered, sir."

I, very much in my element, responded in a

quiet, serene voice, "Very well. Fire."

The *Excalibur* shuddered in response as its arsenal roared to life. The ship shuddered with action, plasma cannon firing, missiles launching, and lasers blasting. Twin pulse energy bolts shot toward their closest aggressor, scoring a heavy blow against its armored flank. A plume of debris flared out as secondary systems sparked and died.

The *Excalibur* has scored multiple violent hits on the lead ship.

The second ship, however, launched a salvo of missiles.

Soon, I heard, "Incoming missiles!" from the sensor operator.

"Helm, hard to port."

The *Excalibur* lurched. The crew braced against the sudden change in trajectory.

"Steadman, release jammers and decoys."

My voice was composed and steady. No hint of doubt or worry showed.

A moment later, I said, "Fire anti-missiles."

I knew what was necessary, and I believed in myself.

The entire bridge sensed my strength and drew from it. They performed with a precision that might have been a parade drill.

The lead alien vessel pulsed with a menacing energy flow. A spear of energy lanced out, a blinding flash that grazed their shields, sending a tremor through the ship.

"Shields at 90%!" Master Chief Kovalenko's

voice cut through the rising chaos.

The incoming missiles exploded everywhere except where the Excalibur was. We suffered only one near miss.

As the *Excalibur* maneuvered to avoid the onslaught of enemy fire, I looked around at the faces of my crew. Their eyes were filled with determination, and I felt a surge of resolve. I might not be the real Elias Thorne, but at this moment, I was their captain, and I was the man they need.

I ordered, "Continue fire; target the weapons array of the first ship again."

Steadman said, "Analyzing firing patterns...yes, there!"

The other vessel was maneuvering.

The *Excalibur* once more unleashed its fury. Lasers lanced out; missiles streaked from their bays, weaving a web of destructive energy. The alien ship staggered under the onslaught, shields flaring dangerously.

And then, as quickly as it had started, the battle ended.

Steadman shouted, "Alien vessels are breaking off. They're...retreating?"

The bridge fell into a stunned, happy silence.

Had we done it? Driven back a force that had previously seemed invincible?

Chalamet spoke, a note of dread in her voice. "Sir, I'm getting new readings. Ships...a lot of ships... appearing from further out in the system."

"Brace yourselves," I said grimly. "This fight is

far from over."

As the day wore on, the aliens held their position in the outer regions of the star system.

I said, "Lieutenant Chalamet, I'm sending you for help."

Ayne met my gaze steadily. "Understood, sir. I won't fail."

I handed her a sealed data-chip. "This holds everything we know—alien tech readings, upgrading sensor detection, attack patterns, and the coordinates for the Ross-248 Star. And..." my fingers tightened on the small metal disc, "this personal message for the commanding officer there."

She took it, tucking it securely into her pocket.

I said, "I don't have a proper military ship for you—just a civilian freighter. But you'll need to pull every erg of energy out of her to maximize her speed and get to Ross-248 as quickly as possible. For now, the enemy ships are just sitting at the rim of the star system. They're waiting for something before they move in. I don't know how long that will be. It would help if you got to Ross and back before they obliterate everything in this system. Do you understand?"

"I do, sir."

"You should be fast enough to make it in two weeks. I'll keep the aliens busy here with *Excalibur* as long as possible. I'll be playing for time, Lieutenant."

Ayne nodded, a determined glint in her eye. "I'll

be back with reinforcements."

With a final salute, she turned, disappearing through the airlock.

I thought, *hope is a fragile thing.*

The journey to Ross-248 was a gauntlet of adversity for Lieutenant Ayne Chalamet. The civilian freighter groaned under the strain of its pushed-to-the-limit engines. Ayne, her face set in grim determination, stood on the bridge, her eyes fixed on the starfield stretching endlessly before her.

The makeshift crew, a ragtag assembly of volunteers and last-minute assignees worked tirelessly to keep the ship together. They were a far cry from the well-oiled machine of the Excalibur, but what they lacked in experience they made up for in sheer grit and determination.

Barely a day into their journey, an internal explosion rocked the ship. It sent shudders through the hull and set off a cacophony of alarms. Thrown from her feet, Ayne clawed back to the command chair, barking orders as she went.

"Damage report!" she yelled over the chaos.

"Hull breach in section 12!" came the reply, the voice of the young Midshipman Nicole, who was acting as engineer. Her trembling with barely controlled panic. "Emergency force fields are holding, but we're venting atmosphere."

Chalamet's mind raced, the countless hours

of training and simulations kicking into high gear. "Divert all available power to the containment systems," she commanded, her voice steady despite the hammering of her heart. "And get repair teams down there immediately."

The hours that followed were a blur of frantic activity and desperate improvisation. Suited figures worked in the cold vacuum of space, welding torn metal and jury-rigging bypasses around damaged systems. In the engine room, Nicole fought to keep the overloaded engines from tearing themselves apart.

But even as they battled one crisis, another loomed on the horizon. A cascade failure, triggered by the initial explosion, spread through the ship's systems like a cancer. One by one, crucial components shut down. Finally, with a shudder and a groan, the engines died, leaving them drifting in the void.

Despair threatened to overwhelm Chalamet in that moment. The weight of her mission, the lives that depended on her success, pressed down on her like a physical force. But she pushed it aside, focusing instead on the task at hand.

"We're not done yet," she said, her voice cutting through the gloom over the bridge.

Nicole showed her resilience and fortitude when she said, "We're going to figure this out."

And figure it out. They did. They worked Through long hours, cannibalized non-essential systems for parts, reconfigured power distribution networks, and coaxed every last ounce of performance out of the battered ship.

It was a patchwork solution, held together with little more than hope and determination, but it worked. The engines returned online, the hull held, and the ship approached Ross-248.

When they finally arrived, Chalamet was running on little more than adrenaline and sheer stubborn will. Her uniform was stained and tattered, her face gaunt with exhaustion.

Two weeks after she began, Chalamet stood on the bridge of the vast military carrier, *Orion*, orbiting the Ross-248 Star. Its sleek design and the intimidating array of weaponry were a world away from the cramped freighter that had brought her.

"Lieutenant Chalamet," a gruff voice boomed across the bridge, "Report."

Rear Admiral Davenport was a towering figure, his uniform ribbons gleaming under the harsh artificial light. Ayne squared her shoulders, and her travel-worn uniform felt faded in comparison.

"Sir, I have urgent dispatches from the Cygni System." She extended the data-chip and the small metal disc I had entrusted to her. "Captain Elias Thorne requests immediate assistance. Hostile alien forces..."

"Let me see that," said Davenport as he snatched the items from her. His brow furrowed as he scanned the initial reports. Then his fingers closed around the metal disc, and just for a moment, his stern facade cracked as he read the message.

From: Captain Elias Thorne, SOS

To: Commanding Officer, Ross-248 Star System

Subj: Hostile Aliens attacking Cygni Star System

Reference (a) Upon First Contact with Hostile Aliens

In accordance with Reference (a), *Excalibur* has taken a defensive posture in the Cygni System.

Need immediate assistance.

Send help.

Elias Thorne
Captain Elias Thorne, *Excalibur*
Special Operations Service

Davenport looked up, a fire in his eyes. "Call an immediate meeting of all flag officers," he barked at his chief of staff.

Then he turned back to Chalamet. "Lieutenant, standby. We leave within the hour."

A surge of joy washed away her exhaustion. "Yes, sir!"

However, the admiral looked as if he had seen a ghost.

He rasped, "Elias Thorne!"

CHAPTER 19

Gathering Storm

*O*rion emerged from hyperspace like a goliath breaching the surface of a cosmic ocean.

"Send out scouts," Davenport ordered, his voice cutting through the anticipation that hung over the bridge.

An hour later, the scouts reported a scene of desperation. The *Excalibur* was facing off against a huge enemy fleet. Neither side was advancing, but once Davenport's fleet approached, the aliens turned and left the region.

Admiral Davenport's eyes were alight with fire, and he wasted no time. "I want eyes on those alien ships. Follow them, learn everything you can," he barked, his voice cutting through the excited chatter on *Orion's* bridge.

Then he added, "Launch the fighters," though he harbored little hope they would catch the enemy.

The recon ships used the hastily developed

detection gear that I had specified. Then, sleek and silent, they slipped from *Orion's* bay, ghosting after the enemy fleet in stealth mode. They danced at the edge of sensor range, their advanced scanners probing and dissecting every scrap of data they could glean from the alien vessels.

As the days passed, a picture began to emerge. The retreating alien ships headed towards their home base. It was a sprawling complex nestled in the heart of a dense asteroid field on the outskirts of the nearby Krugar-60 system.

This star system, a binary star system on the fringes of human-controlled space, had always been a quiet, unremarkable corner of the galaxy. But now scans revealed a hive of activity. There were repair docks, weapons platforms, and a myriad of smaller craft swarming like angry bees.

But the planets beyond the base truly captured the attention of the recon crews. A string of three worlds, each teeming with life and industry, stretched out in the void. These were no mere outposts. They were full-fledged colonies, the beating heart of an alien empire that had, until now, remained hidden from human eyes.

The main military base was on the third planet with multiple battle stations orbiting and a large fleet in support.

The implications were staggering. This was not

a mere raiding party or an isolated skirmish. It was the first contact with a civilization. One that was vast and powerful, and apparently been watching humanity's progress with wary eyes for a long time.

I stood on *Excalibur's* bridge, my uniform crisp, and my demeanor calm, belying the turmoil within me.

The viewscreen flickered to life, revealing the stern visage of Admiral Davenport. His salt-and-pepper hair and sharp eyes exuded authority, and his voice boomed through the speakers. "Captain Thorne, report aboard the Orion."

I swallowed hard—my mouth suddenly dry. "Aye aye, Admiral."

Orion's sleek hull dwarfed the Excalibur. It only took a few minutes before I stood at attention in Admiral Davenport's flag office.

The Admiral's gaze swept over me, taking my measure.

"Captain Thorne," Davenport said, his tone clipped and formal. "We have much to discuss, but I must admit, I was expecting someone..."

As Davenport's words hung in the air, I felt a flicker of self-doubt. I had fought so hard to maintain the illusion of Captain Thorne, to live up to the legend I had unwittingly inherited. But now, faced with the piercing gaze of a seasoned admiral, I couldn't help but wonder if my deception was crumbling.

"Older, sir?" I finished, a wry smile tugging at the corners of my mouth.

Davenport's eyes narrowed. "More experienced. Your reputation precedes you, Captain, but I find it hard to reconcile the stories with the man standing before me."

I met the admiral's gaze unflinchingly. "I assure you, sir, the stories are just that—stories. What matters now is the crisis at hand."

Davenport grunted a noncommittal sound that could have been agreement or disdain. "Indeed, Captain."

Davenport's voice took on a tone of brusque efficiency as he stood up and took a step forward. "I've reviewed your report, and while I commend your efforts thus far, I believe a more direct approach is necessary. I propose to attack the enemy base."

I frowned. "With respect, Admiral, we still know very little about the enemy's capabilities. Rushing into a confrontation could be . . . disappointing."

Davenport leaned forward and said, "And waiting for them to make the first move could be even more so. The sudden arrival of my fleet gives us the element of surprise. They couldn't have expected such a strong force to come here so quickly."

Davenport's expression hardened and his jaw clenched. "Time is a luxury we don't have, Captain. Every moment we delay, the aliens grow stronger and more entrenched. We must strike Kruger now."

My mind raced, searching for a way to dissuade

the admiral from his course of action. "Sir, I urge you to reconsider. My crew and I have been studying the Krug technology, and we believe—"

"Your crew," Davenport interrupted, "will follow orders. As will you, Captain."

I opened my mouth to argue, but something in Davenport's gaze stopped me. There was a fire there, a determination that bordered on obsession. I realized with a sinking feeling that the admiral's mind was made up.

My jaw clenched, but I remained silent. Davenport's gaze softened fractionally.

"I understand your concerns, Captain, but I do not believe in hesitation." He paused for a long moment while he examined my equally determined face.

"However," he said, seemingly to back down a peg. "I will consult with all my senior officers before deciding."

CHAPTER 20

Reckoning

Within the sanctuary of the Kruger nebula, the OV'aa council hummed with a cold, calculating fury. The main holoscreen displayed the aftermath of the recent battle. The smoldering damaged two warships were limping back to the cloaked OV'aa fleet.

Xi'ara's voice echoed through the chamber, resonating with barely contained rage. "These humans...their audacity is astounding!"

She considered the implications of the humans' victory. In all her centuries of leadership, she had never encountered a species so resilient, so quick to adapt. A part of her, buried deep beneath the layers of cold pragmatism, couldn't help but feel a flicker of admiration for their tenacity. But she quashed the thought as quickly as it had come. Admiration was a luxury she could not afford, not when the very future of the OV'aa was at stake.

"And their actions were entirely illogical,"

rasped Councilor N'kala, his bioluminescence pulsing with agitation. "A desperate, seemingly futile act."

"Yet they succeeded!" Xylia hissed, "We underestimated them. This lone ship inflicted severe damage on two battlecruisers. Imagine what a fleet of such…determined warriors could achieve."

"It was a fluke," said Admiral Zo'axa. "By charging directly at our ships, the enemy was able to penetrate the envelope of our superior long-range weapons. Consequently, the resulting short-range weapons exchanges were more favorable to them. We shall not allow such a tactic to occur int eh future."

"But how did the enemy guess that that was our most vulnerable point?"

A silence settled over the council. It was true, the battle had been a humiliating setback.

"The Cygni facility must be dealt with swiftly," Xi'ara declared, her bioluminescent markings flaring with resolve. "Prepare the dreadnaughts. It is time to demonstrate the true extent of our power. No more half-measures."

The OV'aa fleet, previously lurking in the shadows, began to mobilize. Gleaming warships detached from their cloaked positions. They formed an armada that dwarfed their scouting force. At its center was the Leviathans, the OV'aa dreadnaughts—gargantuan vessels armed with weapons capable of reducing entire planets to cinders.

"We cannot allow these humans to disrupt our operations further," Xylia hissed. "This enemy will make an instructive example."

Xi'ara's nod was a chilling pronouncement. "And when their spirit is broken and their defiance is ground to dust, the rest of humanity will learn to fear us. The Cygni system shall belong to the OV'aa, and none shall dare to challenge our dominion."

CHAPTER 21

Gold Braid

*O*rion's ready room was filled with the captains of the fleet. The leaders included Captains Wells of the battlecruiser Invincible and Johnson of the Courageous. They occupied the front seats—the captains of the cruisers, destroyers, and support ships filled in behind them. At the back of the room, the civilian captains of tankers, cargo ships, transports, and space tugs took their seats. The room glittered with gold braid. Furtive glances darted between the various ship commanders. As representatives of Janus' interests, Kate Halliday and Austin Harrison sat in the front row.

Orion's ready room was a circular chamber designed to accommodate large gatherings. The walls were lined with sleek, black panels that displayed real-time data from various ship systems, casting a soft, blue glow throughout the room. A massive holographic projection dominated the front. Its surface was currently displaying a detailed image of the Cygni system. The captains and civilian leaders were seated in comfortable chairs. The atmosphere was charged with tension.

Admiral Davenport stood at the podium, facing the assembled military and civilian leaders. The faces around the room reflected a mixture of uncertainty and impatience.

"Officers and leaders of the Cygni system, welcome!" Davenport announced in a booming voice. His eyes swept the room. "The appearance of aliens has caused understandable alarm, but I am confident that we can provide security and victory for the Imperium over the Krug."

An uncomfortable stir rippled through the room, and murmurs of concern about the alien threat could be heard.

Davenport raised his hands to quiet the audience. "The Krug threat is indeed daunting. Their cruiser-destroyer squadrons have launched raids throughout the system. They have done considerable damage to our outposts and interfered with local shipping. We have been conducting reconnaissance of their main fleet."

I, sitting near the front, stood up. "Admiral, if I may?"

Davenport looked displeased at the interruption, but since I was an SOS captain, I outranked all other captains in the room.

He said, "Captain Thorne, make your statement."

I said, "I believe we should exercise caution and patience. Too much about these aliens remains unknown. We don't know how many star systems they inhabit or which ones. We have only a few examples of their weapons systems. There may be more. It is possible they may have many more fleets hidden behind this vanguard."

Davenport's brow furrowed. "And what do you propose, Captain Thorne?"

I said, my voice calm but firm, "I suggest we send word to the Imperium on Earth, focus on defending Janus, and send stealth scout ships to gather more intelligence before launching any major offensive."

A murmur of both agreement and dissent rippled through the room. Davenport's lips tightened. "Typical of SOS to prefer surveillance over action," he muttered under his breath.

I pressed on. "The Excalibur has superb stealth abilities, which can be further enhanced by the work of Dr. Haliday's team."

Kate rose and said, "That's true. I'm sure we can improve on the existing system."

I said, "Thank you Dr. Haliday. We will count on you."

I continued, "We could use this advantage to infiltrate the alien occupied Kruger-60-star system and gather critical intelligence. We could learn about their technology, military strength, and home world."

Some captains nodded, while others looked skeptical. Captain Wells spoke up. "I, for one, would regret moving in a rather hasty manner."

The debate continued, with captains expressing

opposing and supporting views. I argued for a measured, intelligence-driven approach. Davenport and some more hawkish captains continued to push for immediate, decisive action.

As the meeting stretched on, my hands clenched beneath the table. I remained outwardly tranquil, but inwardly, I was growing impatient.

To Davenport's surprise, most captains finally sided with my more cautious approach.

Davenport said, "Very well. We will proceed as Captain Thorne suggests. But mark my words, I will not delay action indefinitely. Once we've gathered critical data, we will attack."

I nodded, a flicker of relief in my eyes. "Understood, Admiral. The Excalibur will begin preparations for an intelligence-gathering mission immediately."

Davenport said, "Lucky for you, Captain Thorne, I brought a squad of SOS from Ross-248 with the fleet."

I froze.

"You can use them to set up a surveillance outpost in Kruger-60. Sergeant Simpson is anxious to meet with you."

Me?!

CHAPTER 22

Unmasked

As the war effort intensified, Kate became torn between her dedication to dark matter research and the urgent need for her expertise in developing stealth technology. The once-pristine labs of the Janus facility were now cluttered with schematics, prototypes, and the residue of round-the-clock work.

Kate stood hunched over a workbench, her eyes straining as she pored over the latest sensor data. The numbers blurred before her, a testament to the endless hours she had spent trying to coax just a little more efficiency out of the cloaking systems.

Over the next few days, engineers and technicians worked around the clock to fabricate the new components. Programmers honed the software to integrate the cloak into *Excalibur's* existing systems.

Kate oversaw every aspect of the process. Her keen eye for even the slightest imperfections. Her quick mind devised solutions to problems. She barely slept, subsisting on a steady stream of coffee and the adrenaline of creation.

"Kate?" a voice called behind her, startling her.

She turned to see Harrison, his usually bright eyes dulled by fatigue and worry.

"Hey," she said, forcing a smile. "What's up?"

Harrison sighed, running a hand through his messy hair. "I just got word from the *Excalibur*. They need the upgraded stealth modules by tomorrow. Admiral's orders."

Kate's shoulders sagged. "Tomorrow? But we're still running simulations. We need more time to ensure the stability of the sensors."

"I know," Harrison said, "But time is a luxury we don't have. The Krug fleet is moving, and our ships need every advantage."

Kate closed her eyes. When she agreed to help with the war effort, she had never imagined it would completely consume her life. The dark matter research, once her driving passion, was slipping further away each day.

"What are we doing, Harrison?" she asked, her voice barely above a whisper. "We're scientists, not weapons designers. I feel like we're losing ourselves in all of this."

Harrison was silent for a long moment. When he finally spoke, his voice was heavy with understanding. "I know what you mean. It's like we've been swept up in something. But Kate... what we're doing here, it matters."

Kate opened her eyes, meeting Harrison's gaze. She saw the same conflicting emotions that warred within her.

"I just... I can't help but wonder if we're on the right path," she confessed. "If by focusing so much on this war, we're losing sight of why we became scientists in the first place."

Harrison reached out, placing a comforting hand on her shoulder. "I understand, Kate. Truly, I do. But right now, the best thing we can do, the most important thing... is to ensure a future for our research. And that means doing everything in our power to help win this war."

Kate took a deep breath, letting Harrison's words sink in. He was right, of course. The dark matter research would mean nothing if the alien threat consumed them all. But still, a part of her mourned for the purity of scientific discovery.

"Okay," she said at last, squaring her shoulders. "Let's get these stealth modules ready. But Harrison... promise me something?"

"Anything," he replied without hesitation.

"When this is over, we'll return to our true work. We'll dive back into the mysteries of dark matter, and we won't look back."

Harrison smiled a genuine smile that chased away the shadows in his eyes. "I promise, Kate."

The next day, Kate Haliday stood in the heart of

the Janus research facility. Her eyes were fixed on the holographic schematics floating before her. The sleek lines of the *Excalibur* rotated slowly, every curve and angle laid bare in shimmering blue light. Around her, the hum of machinery and the low murmur of voices filled the air as her team worked tirelessly to bring their latest innovation to life.

I stood beside her, his gaze equally focused on the projection. "I have to admit, I'm impressed," he said. I didn't think improving *Excalibur's* stealth capabilities this much was possible."

Kate allowed herself a small smile. "Never underestimate the power of a determined group of scientists," she replied. "We've been working around the clock to redesign the cloaking system. We've incorporated some of the insights we've gained from our dark matter research and your exchange with the aliens."

She gestured to the holograph, which zoomed in on the ship's outer hull. "The key is in the new meta-electro-dark fields we've developed. They're capable of bending light and other electromagnetic waves around the ship. It renders it virtually invisible to most forms of detection."

My eyebrows rose. "Most forms?"

Kate nodded. "There are always limits, even with the most advanced technology. The cloak is most effective against long-range sensors, but the distortions become more noticeable as you get closer. You could be unmasked at a range of less than one light-minute."

I frowned. "That could be a problem in close-quarters engagements."

"It's a trade-off," Kate acknowledged. "But we've also improved the ship's electronic warfare suite. The new countermeasures should help to compensate for any shortcomings in the cloaking system."

She swiped her hand, and the hologram shifted, revealing the *Excalibur's* power distribution network. "There's one more thing you need to be aware of," she said, her tone turning serious. "The cloak is incredibly power-hungry. You'll need to divert energy from non-essential systems to maintain integrity when stealth is active."

My frown deepened. "Define 'non-essential.'"

"Anything that's not critical to the ship's basic functioning and life support," Kate replied. "Comfort systems, certain scientific instruments, even some weapons. You'll need to prioritize."

She could see the wheels turning in my head as he processed this information. "And what about speed?" I asked.

"The faster you go, the more strain you put on the cloak," Kate explained. "We recommend limiting your speed to one-third of the maximum when the stealth system is engaged. Any faster, and you risk creating noticeable distortions in the space-time fabric."

I was silent for a long moment, his gaze distant. Kate could almost see him running through scenarios in his mind, weighing the advantages and limitations of the new technology.

Finally, I nodded. "It's a calculated risk," he said, "but one I'm willing to take. The ability to move unseen could give us a critical edge in future battles."

Kate felt a swell of pride. "We'll do everything in our power to ensure you have that edge," she promised.

Finally, the upgrades were installed. Kate stood on the observation deck, watching as the *Excalibur* gleamed with promise.

I said, "I don't know how to thank you."

Kate turned to me, her heart racing at the intensity of my gaze. "Just promise me one thing," she said, her voice barely above a whisper.

"Anything," I replied, my hand finding hers and intertwining our fingers.

"Come back to me," Kate said, her throat tight with emotion. "No matter what happens out there, no matter what you face... come back to me."

My grip tightened, and I drew her close. "Always," I promised. "I'll always come back to you."

And with those words, sealed with a kiss, I set forth on *Excalibur*.

CHAPTER 23

SOS

I had put off this meeting for as long as possible. Varek stood beside me at the airlock to greet Sergeant Simpson and the SOS squad.

My heart was pounding as I took a deep breath, steeling myself for the encounter.

The airlock hissed open, revealing a group of men and women clad in the distinctive black and gold uniforms of the Special Operations Service.

At their head stood Paul Simpson, a tall, broad-shouldered man with a chiseled jaw and piercing blue eyes. He snapped to attention as I approached, his gaze filled with respect and anticipation.

Simpson, his eyes focused on the older, more seasoned appearing Varek, said in a deep, resonant voice, "Captain Thorne, it's an honor to finally meet you, sir. Your reputation precedes you."

I forced a smile. My mouth was suddenly dry. "The honor is mine, Sergeant." Simpson turned his gaze to me as I continued, "I've heard great things about your squad."

Simpson recovered his composure and beamed with pride. "We're the best of the best, sir. Ready to follow you into the jaws of hell itself."

I nodded, feeling a twinge of guilt at my deception, and no little concern for Varek to witness the event.

"I have no doubt," I said, my voice steady. "And I'm afraid I'm going to have to ask you to do just that."

Simpson's eyes widened, a flicker of excitement crossing his face. "Of course, sir. Whatever the mission, we're ready."

I gestured for the squad to follow me, leading them through the winding corridors of the *Excalibur*. As we walked, I couldn't help but notice the curious glances and whispered comments from my crew. The presence of the SOS squad was a reminder of the dangerous waters we were navigating and the high stakes of our mission.

Finally, we reached the briefing room. I motioned for the squad to take their seats, then activated the holographic display in the center of the table.

Varek took his leave to attend other duties.

I was glad to see him go.

"Your mission," I began, my voice grave, "is to establish a clandestine outpost in the Kruger-60 system. From there, you will gather intelligence on the alien forces, their capabilities, and their intentions. You will coordinate with the Excalibur which will be operating under stealth in the system."

The squad leaned forward. Their faces were rapt with attention.

"Make no mistake," I continued, "this will be a dangerous assignment. We will be operating deep within enemy territory, with no support and no backup. We will be relying on stealth and guile to avoid detection, and on our wits and training to survive."

Simpson nodded. His expression remained serious. "We understand the risks, sir. But we also understand the importance of this mission. The fate of the Imperium may well rest on the intelligence we gather."

"Indeed, it may," I agreed. "Which is why we must proceed with the utmost caution. Dr. Haliday and her team have been working to enhance *Excalibur's* stealth capabilities, but even with their upgrades, we will be vulnerable if detected."

I brought up a schematic of the Kruger system, highlighting the location of the proposed outpost.

"We will insert via short jumps, using the system's asteroid belt as cover. Once we have established the outpost, we will begin a series of reconnaissance missions. We will deploy passive listening devices to monitor shipping and enemy communications. Data on the aliens' movements, technology, and command structure is vital. Our AI will work to develop a translation of the Krug language as well as crack any encryption."

Simpson studied the schematic; his brow

furrowed in concentration. "What about extraction, sir? If things go south, how do we get out?"

I met his gaze with a grim expression. "We don't. At least not immediately. If compromised, there will be no quick rescue. You will have to survive on your own until the situation offers a possibility of rescue. I have no idea of a time frame for that."

A heavy silence settled over the room as the weight of my words sank in. Finally, Simpson nodded, his jaw set with determination.

"Understood, sir. We knew the risks when we signed up. We're ready to do what needs to be done."

I felt a rush of gratitude for the lieutenant's unwavering loyalty. "Thank you, Simpson. When you came aboard Excalibur, you said you would follow me into the jaws of hell itself."

A broad smile crossed my face as I said, "I'm holding you to it."

I turned to the rest of the squad as they managed to laugh grudgingly.

"We leave in six hours. Get your gear stowed and your affairs in order. We won't be coming back until our mission is complete."

As the squad filed out of the briefing room, I couldn't shake the unease that had settled in the pit of my stomach.

As I returned to the bridge, I overheard snatches of conversation from my crew; their voices tinged with concern and uncertainty.

"SOS? On board the *Excalibur*?"

"I heard they're the best of the best but also the

most ruthless. They'll do whatever it takes to get the job done."

"What are we getting ourselves into?"

CHAPTER 24

Outpost

I sat in the command chair of the Excalibur, my gaze fixed on the viewscreen as the ship moved through space cloaked in a veil of stealth technology. Beside me, Lieutenant Ayne Chalamet monitored the ship's systems.

"Stealth field holding steady," she reported. "We're running silent with all emissions masked."

I nodded. The upgrades Kate and her team had made were working. The ship was now masked by a complex web of gravitational lensing and electromagnetic distortion.

However, I felt a growing sense of unease as we approached the Kruger system.

"Dropping out of warp," helmsman Craig announced. "Entering the system now."

The Kruger-60 twin suns burned fiercely. But it was the planets that captured my attention. A string of planets, each one a glittering jewel. And orbiting each world were the unmistakable signs of a thriving civilization. The vast cities had sprawling industrial complexes, and space elevators rising from the surface. The third planet had a large fleet base.

"A wonder," Chalamet breathed, her eyes wide.

I nodded.

I turned to Sergeant Simpson, who stood at the rear of the bridge, his gaze fixed on the tactical display. "Sergeant, gather your SOS squad. It's time to find a place to set up shop."

Simpson said, "Aye aye, sir. We'll be ready to deploy on your order."

I needed to find a location close enough to the alien worlds to gather intelligence but far enough away to avoid detection.

"There," I said, pointing to a small, irregularly shaped asteroid that tumbled through the system's inner reaches. "That's our spot."

Chalamet nodded. "The composition looks good," she reported. "It's mostly nickel-iron, with some carbonaceous deposits. It should be easy enough to set up a base camp."

I said, "Take us in, nice and easy."

Soon, the SOS squad unloaded their gear from the Excalibur's cargo hold. Crates of supplies, portable shelters, and sophisticated surveillance and communication equipment were carefully stacked. They were secured on the asteroid's rocky terrain.

In the center of the base camp, a small, domed structure rose from the ground. This was the nerve center of the communication operation. The squad would monitor alien communications and analyze the data.

Sergeant Jackson, a grizzled veteran with a face like weathered leather, oversaw the deployment of the passive sensors. These small, unobtrusive devices were carefully placed at strategic locations across the nearby asteroid belt, their delicate antennae tuned to pick up the faintest whisper of Krug transmissions.

"Make sure those solar panels are angled correctly," Jackson barked, his voice carrying across the barren landscape. "We need every ounce of power we can get out here."

The squad worked tirelessly. The solar panels glittered in the light, their blue-tinged surfaces a stark contrast to the dull grey of the asteroid's rocky surface.

As the base camp took shape, Chalamet and I watched from the Excalibur's observation deck, our gazes fixed on the activity below.

"They're doing good work," I murmured. "Simpson and his team know their stuff."

Chalamet nodded, her expression thoughtful. "But the real test is still to come. Once those sensors start picking up alien chatter, we'll have a whole new ballgame."

I knew she was right. The passive sensors were just the first step, gathering intelligence without revealing our presence. But sooner or later, we would have to take a more active role to probe the Krug inner defenses.

Sergeant Simpson hunched over a bank of monitors inside the command dome, his gaze intent as he watched the data stream in from the sensors. The screens were alive with alien chatter, a cacophony of strange, guttural sounds that seemed to pulse with a rhythmic intensity.

"What are we looking at here, Lieutenant?" I asked, my eyes scanning the readouts with a practiced eye.

Simpson shook his head, his brow furrowed in concentration. "It's hard to say, sir. The language is unlike anything I've ever heard. But the patterns... there's a structure there, a logic that we might be able to decipher given enough time."

CHAPTER 25

Bird's Eye View

While the SOS squad outpost gathered system-wide information about the star system from the asteroid belt. I intended to use the Excalibur to explore specific military targets of opportunity. I particularly had my heart set on the military base.

From several million kilometers distance, the *Excalibur* managed a bird's-eye view of the alien's main base. It orbited the Kruger-3, the third planet. There were surrounding orbiting shipyards and space stations, creating a cocoon-like space harbor.

Operating in stealth mode the *Excalibur* approached the outer edge of the nest of battle stations and satellites. I conducted a spiral search to map the interrelated defenses. The crew was excited to penetrate deep into Krug territory.

"We've reached the harbor's maximum missile range, sir," said the officer of the deck.

"Very well," I said. "We'll alter course in a few

minutes. Gather as much data as possible."

The ship moved slowly in stealth mode.

"Aye aye, sir," responded CIC.

Chalamet was hard at work with several CIC techs collecting information about defenses, missile batteries, ships, and base facilities. They noted a space station under construction and the several dozen ships in orbit. Kruger-3's moons were alive, and there were numerous ships traveling among them.

At the outer edges of the harbor, the picket ships patrolled between satellite sensor arrays. Drones moved between the various stations. Since the *Excalibur's* trajectory passed close to many of those guard posts, they would get a real test of their new stealth technology.

A Krug picket ship lumbered close but failed to discover the *Excalibur*. The satellite sensor array likewise failed.

I thought, *our new stealth system is working.*

The navigator said, "We're coming up on a course change."

"Closest approach will occur ninety seconds after we alter course, sir," reported the sensor tech.

"That's inside their effective missile range, sir," said the OOD.

"I hope our intelligence estimates are accurate," I said.

"Me too, Captain," said Varek.

"Very well. Execute course change."

"Aye aye, sir."

The CIC reported that one of the picket ships

altered course in the general direction of the *Excalibur*.

The agile *Excalibur* was prepared to open fire from every laser and plasma battery if it came to that, but her chances of surviving a serious engagement were unrealistic. Despite a moment of concern, the picket moved away, once again failing to detect the *Excalibur*.

"We're slipping passed, sir," reported the sensor tech.

We were now at the threshold of the harbor mouth and had a splendid view of the inner bastion.

"We'll change course while observing their ships," I said. "OOD, come left ten degrees, set course 122, mark three."

"Aye aye, sir."

"CIC, bridge; give me a count of enemy shipping inside the harbor."

After a few minutes, CIC reported, "Bridge, CIC; We can identify 31 warships, sir. Three battle cruisers are in orbit near the space station along with 14 cruisers and a like number of destroyers. There are numerous civilian vessels, and there are 144 transports, mining ships, and cargo ships scattered across the rear area. The remainder includes smaller craft shuttling between the large vessels and the base. There are several markers we can use to identify this region. The beacon marker to starboard will be useful to take our bearings."

"Bridge, CIC; cruiser is closing to starboard."

"That will be the on-station duty cruiser," Varek observed.

"Yes. Let's test our stealth capability by seeing how close we can come," I said. I checked the console, scanning the navigation information available to them and examining their options. On the one hand, I wanted to test their skills; on the other, I didn't want to press his luck. Constant observation and testing would improve their information gathering geometrically as well as our abilities to avoid detection.

"The duty ship seems to be heading in our general direction," said Varek, a drop of sweat dripping down his forehead.

"Bridge, engineering; Captain, you requested to be notified when the stealth charge is depleted to 50 percent, sir. We've reached that point."

"Engineering, bridge; Very well," I said.

"I think we've come close enough," I said to the bridge crew. "Let's back off slowly, Mr. Varek. It's time to head back to base."

While the *Excalibur* maintained its vigilant watch outside the harbor, a *Firebird* ventured deeper into enemy territory, a daring gambit to uncover the secrets of their foe.

Within the cramped craft, Midshipman Angelica Nicole and I worked in perfect harmony. As they approached an enemy satellite, I could sense Nicole's nervousness. It was her first real taste of action.

"Steady," I said, keeping my voice calm and reassuring. "Trust in your training, in the ship. We'll get through this together."

Nicole nodded. Her eyes were bright with determination. "Aye, Captain. I won't let you down."

I knew her expertise as a communication officer would be valuable.

The *Firebird* conducted stealth observations, slipping through the enemy's defenses like a ghost. Nicole diligently recorded every scrap of data they could gather.

But the real challenge lay ahead. To truly understand the enemy's plans, they needed to get close, to tap into the very heart of their communications network.

With bated breath, they brought the *Firebird* near a junction box satellite, a hub of electronic activity that held the key to the alien's secrets.

"Were we detected?" Nicole asked, her voice tight with tension.

I checked the sensors, my brow furrowed in concentration. "I don't know. But we must take the chance. This is too important."

Donning their EVA suits, they exited the *Firebird*, floating in the eerie silence of space. The suits encased them completely, their heads enclosed in helmets, their breathing sustained by short-term oxygen capsules.

It was a risk, a gamble. But I knew that in war, sometimes the greatest dangers held the greatest rewards.

The *Firebird* remained in relative position as they landed on the small communication satellite.

With careful, deliberate movements, they made their way to the communication transmission equipment. My heart pounded in his chest as I planted the bugging devices, each one a lifeline to the SOS base in the asteroid belt.

And then, in a moment of sheer audacity, I stepped out from the shadows and placed a briefcase-sized bomb at the base of the junction box. A failsafe, a way to ensure that only I could recover the equipment if things went wrong.

Once we finished the operation, we were anxious to get back aboard the *Excalibur*.

Soon, however, Nicole ventured out on her own to complete the next mission. She was becoming an expert pilot. Time and again, she danced the dance of stealth and subterfuge, retrieving data, piecing together the puzzle of the enemy's plans.

But for all our efforts, some critical pieces of information remained elusive. The warship movements, the troop deployments... they painted a picture, but it was incomplete, a tapestry with holes waiting to be filled.

After surveilling the Kruger-60 system for nearly a month, I gathered the SOS squad from its outpost and left. When I reached Cygni, I reported to the admiral and turned over my findings to the analysts who got very busy dissecting the data.

CHAPTER 26

Debrief

The debriefing room aboard the *Excalibur* was a stark, utilitarian space. Its walls were lined with monitors displaying real-time data from various ship systems. A long, metal table dominated the center of the room, surrounded by a dozen chairs. Each chair on one side of the table was occupied by a member of the SOS squad, fresh from their mission in the Kruger system.

On the opposite side of the table sat Commander Varek, his posture straight and his gaze sharp as he surveyed the assembled operatives.

"Welcome back," he began, his voice crisp and authoritative. "We are facing an enemy unlike any we've encountered before. An alien race with technology and capabilities that, quite frankly, we barely understand. Your role in gathering intelligence on their activities in the Kruger system was essential to our ongoing efforts. And for that, you have my gratitude and respect."

He paused, letting them drink in the praise.

He said, "Your mission was crucial, and I want to assure you that your written reports have been scrutinized in detail. We have analyzed the collected data and synthesized as much information as possible. Nevertheless, I believe that by speaking to you in person, I may find a few tidbits of valuable information. I'm eager to hear your verbal reports."

He paused, letting his words sink in.

A murmur of acknowledgment rippled through the room as the SOS operatives nodded their heads. Their expressions were a mix of pride and solemnity.

Varek's gaze settled on a young woman with short, spikey hair and a scar running down her left cheek. "Sergeant Simpson, let's start with you. Give me an overview of your team's operations."

Simpson leaned forward, her elbows resting on the table as she spoke. "We established a base camp on the designated asteroid as planned. The first few days were spent setting up our surveillance equipment and getting a lay of the star system. We had to be careful not to draw any unwanted attention."

She paused, her eyes flickering to Varek. "It wasn't easy, sir. The alien activity in the system was intense. Their ships constantly came and went, and their communications chatter was nonstop."

Varek nodded. "And what about their technology? Did you observe anything that could give us an edge?"

Simpson hesitated, glancing at her fellow operatives before responding. "Their ships, sir... are unlike anything I've ever seen. The way they move and the energy signatures they give off."

Varek's eyes narrowed. "Elaborate, Sergeant."

Simpson took a deep breath. "There were times when their ships seemed to...flicker. Like they were there one moment and gone the next, only to reappear somewhere else entirely, and their weapons, sir... we saw them in action during a ship exercise. The raw power they unleashed was staggering."

Varek leaned back in his chair; his fingers steepled in front of him as he processed this information. "Interesting," he murmured, almost to himself.

He turned his attention to a broad-shouldered man with a shaved head and a thick beard. "Corporal O'Connor, what about the alien's satellite operations? Did you observe any weaknesses in their defenses that we could exploit?"

O'Connor shook his head, his expression grim. "Their facilities were heavily fortified, sir. Layered defenses, energy shields, and what looked like automated weapons systems. From what we could see, they're not taking any chances."

Varek's mouth tightened into a thin line.

Then he shifted gears, his tone becoming more conversational. "On another note, I'm curious about your experiences working with Captain Thorne. As you know, he's a bit of an enigma, even within the SOS."

O'Connor let out a low whistle. "That's an understatement, sir," he said with a chuckle. I've heard stories about Captain Thorne that would make your hair stand on end. Like the time he supposedly infiltrated a rebel stronghold single-handedly and took out their entire leadership with nothing but a knife and a pack of explosives."

Varek raised an eyebrow. "And do you believe these stories, Corporal?"

O'Connor shrugged. "Hard to say, sir. Thorne's reputation precedes him, but the man keeps his cards close to his chest."

Sergeant Simpson said, "I've heard that he once went undercover as a gang leader just to take down their operation from the inside. They say he's got a talent for becoming anyone he needs to be."

Varek leaned forward. His interest seemed piqued. "A man of many faces, then?"

Simpson nodded. "That's the rumor, sir. But you know how it is with the SOS. The truth is often stranger than the stories."

Varek turned toward a wiry man with sharp features and intelligent eyes. "What about you, Corporal Nguyen? Have you had any direct interactions with Captain Thorne?"

Nguyen hesitated. His brow furrowed in thought. "Not directly, sir. But I did overhear something odd during our mission."

Varek's gaze intensified. "Go on."

"It was during a comm check with the Excalibur. I was monitoring the frequencies and picked up a snippet of a conversation between Captain Thorne and an unknown individual. They were discussing something called 'Operation Raja.'"

Varek's eyes widened almost imperceptibly. "'Operation Raja'? Did you hear anything else?"

Nguyen shook his head. "No, sir. The transmission was cut after that. But the way they were talking sounded like something big, something secret."

An uneasy silence settled over the room as Varek absorbed this information.

Operation Raja.

The name meant nothing to Varek, but the mere fact that Thorne was involved suggested it was significant.

He made a mental note to investigate further as he returned to the squad. "Thank you all for your candor and your service. The information you've provided will be invaluable as we plan our next move."

He stood, signaling the end of the debriefing. "Get some rest, all of you. We have a long fight ahead of us."

As the SOS operatives filed out of the room, Varek remained seated, his mind racing with the implications of what he had learned.

Thorne's mysterious background, reputation for deception, and now this enigmatic Operation Raja all added up to a puzzle that Varek was determined to solve.

He knew that secrets could be as deadly as any weapon in the shadows of war. And he would not rest until he had uncovered the truth behind the man called Elias Thorne.

CHAPTER 27

Strategic Divide

The *Orion's* Admiral cabin was a stark contrast to my utilitarian quarters of the Excalibur. Polished wood paneling and plush carpets exuded an air of luxury. An expansive viewport offered a breathtaking view of the stars beyond. In the center of the room, a large, ornate desk dominated the space. Its surface was cluttered with computer screens showing strategic maps and data analysis.

Admiral Davenport sat behind the desk. His piercing blue eyes were fixed on me as I stood before him. As SOS Captain Thorne, I outranked all the other captains in the fleet and was de facto Davenport's second in command.

"Captain Thorne," Davenport began in a deep voice, "I've summoned you here to discuss the alien threat."

I nodded. I kept my expression guarded. "Of course, Admiral. What do you have in mind?"

Davenport leaned forward, his elbows resting

on the desk. "I intend to send the *Excalibur* and a few destroyers to launch a feint on the enemy's asteroid bases."

I furrowed my brow. "The asteroid bases? With all due respect, Admiral, those installations are heavily fortified. We'd be risking significant losses in order to cause them pain."

A slight smile tugged at the corner of Davenport's mouth. "That's precisely the point, Captain. We need to bait the alien fleet away from their planet and draw them out into the asteroid belt."

"And then what?" I asked, a hint of skepticism in my tone.

"Once their fleet is engaged chasing you in the asteroids, I will lead the *Orion* and the rest of our forces in an all-out assault on their main planet and military base."

My eyes widened. "You want to split our forces? Admiral, with all due respect, that's a dangerous gamble."

Davenport's gaze hardened. "It's a calculated risk, Captain. When the aliens realize their home world is under attack, they'll have no choice but to turn back. And that's when I'll strike."

He stood up, his tall frame imposing as he walked around the desk. "I'll have fighter-bombers waiting in the wings, ready to harass their fleet as they make the long journey back to their planet. By the time they reach us, they'll be decimated, easy pickings for *Orion* and her battle group."

I considered the plan and the forces available:

EARTH IMPERIUM—3rd Fleet
Admiral Davenport
 Spacecraft Carrier—*Orion*
 36 Fighters
 48 Bombers
 6 Recon
Battlecruisers—Invincible, Indominable
12 Cruisers
48 Destroyers
 2 Stealth Recon
12 Auxiliary Support Ship

Sergeant Simpson
Special Operations Service—*2nd Squad*

Krug—Battle Fleet
 4 Dreadnought
 6 Battlecruisers
 36 Cruisers
 88 Destroyers
 88 Auxiliary Support Ships

Planet Kruger-3
20 Battle stations
200 Planetary missile batteries.

I had to admit that the admiral's plan had merit, but I shook my head, my jaw clenched. "Admiral, I must strongly advise against this course of action."

Davenport raised his eyebrows. "Oh? And why is that, Captain?"

I calmly marshalled my thoughts. I visualized a

coherent response that would make my main point. "Attacking heavily fortified battle stations will deplete your resources. It will weaken you before the fleets engage," I explained, my voice steady and controlled. "And, I don't believe the fighter-bombers have enough firepower to inflict critical damage on the alien fleet."

I took a step forward, my gaze intense. "If we proceed with this plan, we risk the enemy reaching your fleet with their strength largely intact. They could deal a devastating blow; one we might not recover from."

Davenport's eyes narrowed, a flicker of annoyance crossing his features. "Captain Thorne, I appreciate your input, but I think you're failing to see the bigger picture here."

He clasped his hands behind his back, his posture straight and unyielding. "This is an opportunity to strike a decisive blow against the Krug infrastructure, to cripple their ability to wage war against us."

My frustration was evident, but I kept my composure. "Admiral, I understand the appeal of a bold, aggressive strategy, but we must weigh the risks. If we underestimate the enemy's resilience and adaptability, we could be walking into a trap of our own making."

Davenport's patience was wearing thin. "I've heard enough, Captain. I'm the commanding officer of this fleet, and I have made my decision."

He fixed me with a steely gaze. "You may be a fair tactician, Thorne, but I am an expert carrier strategist. I know what needs to be done to win this war."

I stood my ground, my voice low and measured. "Admiral, I implore you to reconsider. We have an opportunity to gather more intelligence, to find a weakness in the enemy's defenses that we can exploit."

Davenport waved a dismissive hand. "We don't have the luxury of time, Captain. Every moment we delay, the aliens grow stronger, more entrenched."

He returned to his desk, his fingers tapping impatiently on the polished surface. "You have your orders, Thorne. The *Excalibur* and her escort will lead the attack on the asteroid bases. The rest of the fleet will stand ready to strike when the moment is right."

My shoulders sagged almost imperceptibly, the weight of the Admiral's decision settling upon me. "Aye aye, Admiral."

Davenport's expression softened slightly. "Despite your reservations, Captain, I expect you to carry out your instructions forcefully.

I hesitated for only a moment before I said, "Aye aye, sir."

As the doors to the Admiral's cabin slid shut behind me, I squared my shoulders, my jaw set with fierce determination.

CHAPTER 28

Farewell

I walked up the stone pathway to Kate's home in Newville. It was a simple colonial style two-story house on the road with similar wooden cottages. A veranda overlooked the surrounding flowerbed and well-pruned shrubbery.

Despite its rustic appearance, the house boasted sophisticated in-home AI technology. When I knocked, the door scanned me, recognized me, and automatically opened.

As Kate appeared, I couldn't help but notice the way the soft light from the windows played across her features. Her hair, usually pulled back in a practical ponytail, now fell in loose waves around her face, framing her delicate cheekbones and the curve of her neck. Despite the somber occasion, there was a glimmer of warmth in her eyes, a reminder of the connection we shared.

"I hope I'm welcome?"

"Of course, you're welcome," she leaned

forward and gave me a peck on the cheek. "I'm even ready to forgive you for your unforgivable absence."

I brightened. "I could ask for no more."

As we stood in the living room, the scent of freshly brewed coffee wafted in from the kitchen, mingling with the delicate aroma of the flowers in the nearby vase. The soft hum of the air conditioning unit provided a soothing background noise, a stark contrast to the heavy silence that hung between us.

"I've missed you," she said.

Then for a long moment, we remained silent.

She said, "You're leaving again, aren't you?"

I frowned.

"So soon?"

"It's not my desire, but it's necessary."

Kate eyes filled with a tumultuous mix of anxiety and love.

We stood mere inches apart, the space between us charged with unspoken emotions.

Her gaze searched my face, seeking reassurance, seeking a promise that she knew I couldn't give.

"I..." Kate began, her voice catching in her throat. She took a deep breath, steadying herself before continuing. "I've tried to be strong, to focus on my work and not let the fears consume me. But every time you leave, a part of me wonders if it will be the last time I see you. I can't keep living with this uncertainty, this constant dread that the next knock on my door will be someone telling me you're gone."

I reached out, my fingers brushing her cheek with a tenderness that belied the chaos surrounding us. "Kate, I know it's hard. But I will come back to you, just as I have now. You have to trust in that, in us."

Kate wrung her hands and said, "I have something to tell you."

I waited, but after a long moment, I asked, "What is it, Kate?"

"I'm leaving Janus. I intend to go back to Earth on the next transport."

Surprised and hurt, I took her hands and asked, "Why? I don't understand."

"I want to continue my work—away from this war zone."

I said, "I want you to trust that everything will be all right. You don't have to leave. You can wait here and still be safe while you finish your research."

"I can't. I won't. You have no right to ask that of me."

"Will you wait until I return?"

"Can you offer me something more to hope for?"

I winced. I knew I couldn't.

"Please wait," I pleaded, holding her hand.

"No. You're too late. I can't do my science in the middle of a war. I won't change my mind. I understand your desire, your passion for me, but that's not enough for a commitment. I need security, not a series of visits from an occasional lover."

She pulled her hand away. "I intend to return to Earth."

The thought of losing her struck me like a physical blow. I grasped her arm, and without meaning to, squeezed.

"Don't, you're hurting me. I'll make my own decisions."

"But you love me."

"I did, but I fall in love too easily," she said.

Kate's breath hitched. A single tear escaped and rolled down her cheek. "What if the war takes you from me, forever?"

I listened to her words, each one pounding me. I wanted nothing more than to gather her in my arms, to promise her that everything would be alright, that I would always come back to her. But even as the words formed on my tongue, I knew they would be a lie. The truth was, I couldn't make that promise, no matter how desperately I wanted to.

"I have a part to play in this war," I said. "I can't just think of myself, or even you."

"Then go," she said. "Go! But don't look back because I won't be here."

She wiped her tears away. "I've had my romantic adventure. You were part of it, but now I must have a future. I don't regret loving you, but I can't go on loving you."

My head drooped, I said, "I must go, but I won't give you up."

Kate touched my cheek. "Don't look so sad."

She drew a breath and shrugged as if she were slipping a coat off her shoulders. "I must be practical with my future."

Then, she added more forcibly, "Go! Forget me."

Her words stung. "Kate . . ."

The look on my face softened her heart. She

gave me a small smile and kissed me gently on the lips. Then, she said, "Goodbye," and turned away.

I whispered back, "Goodbye, my love."

But I knew I would see her again.

I can't go on living without seeing her again.

CHAPTER 29

Feint

I sat in his cabin. I fixed my eyes on the holographic display before me. The asteroid bases of the alien bases rotated slowly, their fortifications and defenses laid bare. I called Lieutenants Chalamet, Chen, Steadman, and Midshipman Nicole to my quarters. They squeezed into the small space and stood before me. Their faces were a mix of anticipation and apprehension.

"As you know," I began, keeping my voice steady despite the difficulty of the plan I was about to unveil. "Admiral Davenport has ordered us to launch an assault on the enemy's asteroid bases. It's a daring move, one that could turn the tide of this war if we succeed."

I paused, my gaze sweeping over the assembled officers. "But it's also a move that comes with great risk. During our surveillance of the Kruger star system, we accumulated a great deal of information. We found that the alien defenses in the asteroid belt were formidable. A direct assault could result in heavy losses for our task force."

Steadman leaned forward. His brow was furrowed. "What are you proposing, Captain?"

I tapped a command on my console, and the hologram zoomed in on a specific section of the asteroid field. "To ensure the success of our attack, we need to take out these satellite missile launchers first." He pointed to the red dots in the asteroid field. "Once that is accomplished, we can launch a long-range missile strike on the bases, targeting their critical infrastructure and command centers."

Chalamet's eyes widened. "A commando raid?"

I nodded. "Precisely. Our SOS squad is specifically trained for just such a task. They will infiltrate the missile sites and destroy those launchers, creating a gap in the enemy's defenses that we can exploit."

Nicole stepped forward with her young face showing determination. "What do you need from us, Captain?"

I met her gaze, a flicker of pride and worry warring within me. "Midshipman Nicole, I need you to pilot the transport assault craft that will carry the SOS squad to their target. It's a dangerous mission, one that will require your expert pilot skills. I have faith in your abilities."

Nicole swallowed hard. "I won't let you down, sir."

My expression softened. "I know you won't, Nicole. But I won't lie to you. This mission will put you in harm's way. You'll be flying into the heart of enemy territory. Once your sabotage is complete, you'll extract the squad. Then you'll return to the *Excalibur* in the midst of the battle."

I turned to Chalamet. "Lieutenant, you to coordinate with the SOS squad. Ensure they have all the intel and resources they need to carry out the sabotage. You'll be their lifeline as they hop from one target to another."

Chalamet nodded, her jaw set with resolve. "Understood, Captain. I'll make sure they're prepared for anything."

I said, "Chen you will plot the drop and pickup points for the assault craft. Once the craft is recovered, you will plot the best positions for the *Excalibur* and the destroyers to bombard the military facilities. The constant shifting orbits of asteroids will make that difficult, but I trust you can do it."

"Thank you, sir."

My gaze returned to Nicole, the young midshipman standing tall despite the enormity of the task before her. "Nicole, I won't order you to do this. It's a volunteer mission, and I'll understand if you have reservations."

Nicole shook her head, her eyes bright with a fierce determination. "No reservations, sir. I'm ready to do my part."

A surge of concern and fear mingled in my chest. This young woman, barely out of the academy, was willing to risk everything.

As the briefing concluded, the officers filed out

of his cabin.

In the hangar bay, Nicole stood before the transport assault craft, her flight suit a stark contrast to the gleaming metal around her. The SOS squad was already aboard, their faces grim with the knowledge of the mission ahead.

As she prepared to board, Chief Kovalenko approached, his weathered face etched with concern. "Midshipman Nicole," he said gruffly, his voice low. "Are you sure about this? Flying into the heart of enemy territory, it's no small thing."

Nicole met his gaze, her own eyes clear and steady. "I'm sure, Chief. This is what I trained for, what I signed up for when I joined the fleet."

Kovalenko sighed, his broad shoulders sagging slightly. "I know, lass. But it doesn't make it any easier to watch you go."

He reached out, placing a hand on her shoulder. "Just remember, you've got the best damn ship in the fleet at your back. The *Excalibur* will be watching over you. And so will I."

Nicole nodded, a lump forming in her throat at the chief's words. "Thank you, Chief. I won't let you down."

With a final salute, she turned and boarded the transport. The hatch sealed behind her with a definitive clang. As the craft lifted off, the hangar bay doors slid open, Nicole's heart raced with a mix of fear and exhilaration.

She was flying into a battle that would test her skills and her courage like never before. She revved the engines and the craft lifted off the deck and out if the hanger.

As the transport assault craft hurtled through the asteroid field, Nicole's senses were on high alert. The cockpit was filled with the steady hum of the engines, punctuated by the occasional ping of small debris bouncing off the hull. The recycled air carried a faint scent of sweat and adrenaline, a reminder of the high-stakes mission they were undertaking.

Nicole's hands gripped the controls, her fingers moving with practiced precision as she navigated the treacherous terrain. The asteroids loomed large in the viewscreen, their jagged surfaces casting eerie shadows against the starlight.

"Approaching first drop point," she announced over the comm, her voice steady despite the tension coiled in her gut. "Prepare for deployment."

Sergeant Simpson ordered, "At the ready!"

In the back of the craft, the SOS squad readied their gear, the clank of metal on metal and the snap of buckles filling the air. They were a hardened bunch.

As the transport settled into a hovering position above the first launcher site, Nicole could see the enemy forces scrambling to respond. Laser turrets swiveled in their direction, their barrels glowing with deadly energy. Rail gun emplacements fired, the hypersonic projectiles streaking past the craft with a deafening roar.

"Go, go, go!" Nicole yelled, slamming her fist on the deployment button. The special operations team leaped from the craft, their jetpacks flaring to life as they descended upon the enemy position. The sounds of battle erupted below, the crackle of energy weapons and the boom of explosions echoing through the asteroid field.

Nicole didn't have time to watch the fight unfold. She was already racing to the ready point, her eyes scanning the sensor readings for any sign of enemy reinforcements. The craft shuddered as a laser blast grazed its shields, the acrid scent of burnt circuitry filling the cockpit.

"Shields at 80%," she reported through gritted teeth, her hands moving the controls as she executed evasive maneuvers. The transport whirled and danced through the asteroids, its movements so sudden and erratic that Nicole could feel the G-forces pressing her back into her seat.

Nicole could hear their battle cries over the comm, the sound of warriors giving their all.

One of the squad members took a direct hit from a rail gun, his body flung like a rag doll across the asteroid's surface. Another was pinned down by heavy laser fire, unable to advance or retreat.

"We've got wounded!" the squad leader's voice crackled over the comm, the sound of desperation bleeding through the static. "We need evac, now!"

Nicole's heart pounded in her chest, the weight of the moment pressing down on her like a physical force. She knew that every second counted, that the lives of her comrades hung in the balance.

With a deep breath, she plunged the transport into a steep dive, the craft's engines screaming as she pushed them to their limits. Laser blasts and rail gun slugs filled the air around her, a deadly gauntlet that she navigated with a combination of skill and sheer audacity.

As the transport settled onto the asteroid's surface, the SOS squad rushed to load their wounded comrades. Nicole could see the pain and concern in their eyes, the knowledge that they were leaving no one behind etched into every line of their faces.

"Punch it!" the squad leader Simpson yelled as the last of the wounded were safely aboard. Nicole didn't need to be told twice. With a roar of the engines, the transport leaped into the air, its shields flaring as enemy fire pounded against them.

The journey to the remaining launcher sites was a blur of adrenaline and determination. Nicole flew like a woman possessed, her every movement precise and purposeful. The special operation team fought, their weapons never falling silent as they battled their way from one objective to the next.

In the end, all ten launchers lay in ruins, their crews dead. The transport was battered and scarred; its shields reduced to a flickering whisper.

As Nicole guided the craft back to the *Excalibur*, she reported, "Mission accomplished."

The *Excalibur* surged forward, her engines roaring as she led the charge into the heart of the Kruger-60 asteroid belt. On the bridge, I stood tall, my eyes fixed on the tactical display before him. Beside him, Commander Varek and Lieutenant Chalamet manned their stations. Their faces were etched with grim determination.

"Entering weapons range, Captain," Varek reported.

I nodded. "Engage on my mark, Commander."

Then I sent a message to my destroyer escort, "Commence assault."

The Krug defenses came to life as the four sleek destroyers closed in on the fortified asteroid base. A flurry of plasma fire and missile barrages streaked through the void.

Next, I barked, my eyes narrowing. "Weapons officer, target the power generators and weapons systems. Commence fire."

The *Excalibur's* weapons systems roared to life, with lances of energy and high-yield missiles. They slammed into the enemy's defenses. Explosions blossomed across the asteroid's surface, sending debris and shattered metal spinning into the void. The *Excalibur* weaved and dodged, her shields absorbing the brunt of the onslaught.

From the bridge command console, Master Chief Kovalenko worked frantically to keep the *Excalibur's* systems running.

The battle against the asteroid base intensified. The *Excalibur* and her accompanying destroyers darting in and out of the enemy's fire. They struck hard and fast, targeting the base's critical systems and infrastructure.

As the minutes ticked by, the *Excalibur's* shields began to falter, the constant barrage of enemy fire taking its toll. Kovalenko's voice crackled over the comm, "Captain, shields are at fifty percent and falling."

My mind raced, weighing my options. They had inflicted significant damage on the enemy base, but they were running out of time. If they didn't withdraw soon, they risked severe damage to the *Excalibur* and her escorts.

"Helm, prepare to disengage," I ordered, keeping my voice steady. "On my mark, all back full. We'll regroup."

The small force took a short break, regrouped, and then made a second attack.

We repeated this over the next day until we finally detected the alien fleet heading toward the asteroid belt.

As the *Excalibur* finally moved away from the asteroid base, my thoughts turned to the battle unfolding at the alien home world.

Orion and her battle group had to withstand the full might of the enemy battle stations. I could only pray that Davenport's gambit would pay off.

CHAPTER 30

Mayday

Two light-days away, Admiral Davenport stood on the bridge of Orion, his eyes fixed on the tactical display. The alien fleet had taken the bait. Their dreadnaughts and battlecruisers surged towards the Excalibur in the asteroid belt. It was his turn to strike at the Krug planet and draw the aliens back to base.

"All ships engage the enemy battle stations at will," Davenport ordered, his voice booming across the comm. "Fighter squadrons, begin your attack runs. Let's bring the fight to these alien bastards."

Orion shuddered as it fired its first volley at the enemy battle stations defending the planet. The massive ship's weapons systems were state-of-the-art, designed to deliver maximum damage at extreme range. But even they seemed to barely scratch the surface of the aliens' advanced shielding.

The exchange continued for an entire day. But Davenport's fleet took more damage than he anticipated. The *Orion* and the battlecruisers were forced to move away from the action. Several cruisers and destroyers had to withdraw from the action to tend to serious damage, leaving the remaining ships more vulnerable. The action continued at a high cost.

Finally, Davenport got word that the alien fleet had reached the asteroid belt and was turning around. He broke off the attack on the battle stations and directed his fighter-bombers to strike the alien fleet. The fighter bombers hit the enemy dreadnaughts for an entire day with little success.

The fighter-bombers inflicted some damage on the enemy fleet, but it was clear it would not be enough.

"Admiral, the enemy dreadnaughts are closing fast," Novak warned, his voice tight. "The *Invincible* and the *Indomitable* are taking heavy fire."

Davenport's eyes narrowed, his mind racing. With their advanced shielding and devastating firepower, the alien dreadnaughts were proving to be a formidable foe. The human battlecruisers, for all their might, were struggling to hold the line.

"Concentrate fire on the lead dreadnaught," Davenport ordered, his voice steady. "We need to take out their command ship, disrupt their chain of command. Coordinate with the *Indomitable* and the *Invincible*. We need to take those behemoths down before they tear us apart."

Orion shuddered again as another alien salvo slammed into its shields. On the viewscreen, Davenport could see the *Indomitable* and the *Invincible* moving into position, their weapons systems glowing with barely restrained power.

Orion's weapons systems roared to life, a barrage of high-yield missiles and plasma fire. It slammed into the alien dreadnaught's shields. The massive ship shuddered under the onslaught but continued to press forward. Its own weapons systems flared with a deadly intensity.

There was a lull in the battle as both sides prepared for the next exchange. The alien fleet began to employ a devastating tactic as the battle raged. The dreadnaughts and battlecruisers targeted the human ships' engines. They crippled them with surgical precision.

The *Invincible*, with its engines damaged and hull breached, moved away into the void. The Indomitable, with its shields failing, was swarmed by a dozen enemy cruisers, their weapons tearing through her armor like paper.

On *Orion's* bridge, Davenport watched in growing horror as his fleet was systematically dismantled. The alien dreadnaughts pressed their advantage, unleashing a relentless barrage of fire on his ships. Consoles exploded in showers of sparks, and the screams of the wounded and dying filled the air.

"Admiral, we can't sustain this level of damage," Novak warned, his voice edged with desperation. "We need to withdraw, regroup with the rest of the fleet."

Davenport's jaw clenched. "No. We hold the line, no matter the cost. We cannot let the aliens reach their home world."

Davenport's jaw clenched, his eyes blazing with fierce determination. But he knew that Novak was right, that to stay and fight was to court annihilation.

For a long moment, Davenport was torn between his duty as a commander and his desire to see the mission through to the end. In the end, it was the sight of the *Indomitable*, its once-proud hull now a twisted wreck, which made the decision for him.

"Signal the fleet," he said heavily, his voice thick with emotion. "We're withdrawing. All ships fallback."

But even as he gave the order, Davenport knew that it was too late for many of his ships. The *Invincible* shields were buckling under the unrelenting alien fire. The *Orion* shuddered and groaned as it took hit after hit, its armor buckling and systems failing.

But even as the words left his lips, a massive explosion rocked the *Orion*, sending the bridge crew sprawling. Davenport, thrown from his command chair. He lay listless on the deck, his eyes staring sightlessly at the stars beyond.

Novak, his face ashen, scrambled to the admiral's side. But it was too late. Admiral Davenport, the architect of this bold gambit, was dead.

CHAPTER 31

Darkest Light

I stood on the bridge of the Excalibur as it flew at flank speed to reach the battle.

In the wake of Admiral Davenport's death, he prepared to assume command of the fleet. The once-proud ships had suffered, their crews demoralized in the face of the alien onslaught.

"Lieutenant Chalamet," I said, "Open a fleet-wide channel. I need to address the crews."

Chalamet nodded, her fingers activating the communications console. "Channel open, sir."

I took a deep breath, my mind racing as I tried to find the words that would rally my battered and beaten forces.

"Men and women of the Imperium," I began, forcing my voice to remain steady and resolute. "We have suffered greatly today. Admiral Davenport has fallen in battle against our enemy. His sacrifice will not be forgotten."

I paused, letting my words sink in before continuing. "As ranking Special Operations Service captain, I, Captain Thorne, am assuming command of the fleet. Our priority must be to withdraw to a safe distance and regroup our forces."

I turned to Chen, "Lieutenant, plot a course to position a far enough to give us some breathing room to disengage, but close enough to keep an eye on enemy movements."

Chen nodded; he entered the code into the navigation console. "Course plotted, sir. Ready to transmit on your order."

I turned back to the fleet-wide channel. "All ships regroup on these coordinates and stand by for further orders."

As the fleet acknowledged his command.

Over the next several hours, I worked to bring some semblance of order to the chaos that had engulfed the fleet.

"Their shields are incredibly advanced," Chalamet said, her brow furrowed as she studied the holographic schematics of the alien dreadnaughts. "They seem to be able to adapt to our weapons fire, modulating their frequencies to nullify our attacks."

I nodded grimly. "We need to find a way to pierce those shields, to hit them where they're vulnerable. Otherwise, we'll just be throwing ourselves against a wall."

Chalamet tapped a few commands into the console, bringing up a new set of data. "There might be a way," she said slowly, her eyes narrowing as she studied the readouts. "Our scans of their ships during the battle showed a slight fluctuation in their shield harmonics every time they fired their main weapons. It's almost as if the power drain from their guns creates a momentary weakness in their shield defenses."

I leaned forward, my heart pounding with a sudden surge of hope. "Can we exploit that weakness? Find a way to time our shots to coincide with those fluctuations?"

Chalamet nodded, a small smile playing at the corners of her mouth. "It won't be easy. We'll need to modify our targeting algorithms to take advantage of those shield harmonics. But it's a start."

"There," she said suddenly, pointing to a schematic of one of the alien dreadnaughts. "Their shield harmonics fluctuate every 3.7 milliseconds. If we time our shots right, we might be able to punch through."

CHAPTER 32

Against the Tide

I surveyed the assembled ships. The once-proud fleet, the might of the human Imperium, was badly damaged. The alien fleet, their dreadnaughts, and battlecruisers still bristling with power hung in space, a looming threat that cast a shadow over all who beheld them.

"Lieutenant Steadman," I said, turning to the weapons officer at the tactical station. "I want you to implement a new formation for our fleet. We must maximize our firepower density at the point of attack while maintaining a strong defensive perimeter. And I want you to coordinate firing with Chalamet when she identifies power fluctuation in their shields."

Steadman 's eyes widened, but he nodded. "Aye aye, Captain."

Excalibur and her battered companions licked their wounds and made what repairs they could. They braced themselves for the fight to come. The alien fleet, still flush with victory, remained in open space, a silent challenge to any who would dare face them.

But I knew that we could not afford to wait. Every moment we delayed was another chance for the aliens to regroup, bring in reinforcements, and crush what remained of the human fleet.

"All ships, this is Captain Thorne," I said, his voice ringing across the void. "Assume formation according to the transmitted instructions and prepare to reengage the enemy."

The fleet moved as one, the ships arranging themselves into a tight, concentric defensive ball, with the fighter-bombers nestled in the center of the formation. It was a risky move, one that would leave us vulnerable to a concentrated attack, but it was the only way to ensure that we could bring the full might of their firepower to bear on the enemy.

"Fighter squadrons, your primary objective is to provide close-in defense for the fleet," I ordered, my eyes fixed on the tactical display. "Engage any incoming missiles with antimissiles and keep our ships safe."

As the Krug fleet loomed closer, the *Excalibur's* sensors lit up, detecting the telltale signs of weapon locks, and targeting systems. My heart raced, my palms slick with sweat as I watched the enemy ships close in.

"All ships, open fire at assigned targets!" I commanded, my words ringing out across the bridge.

The human fleet erupted with a barrage of weapons fire, lances of energy, and high-yield missiles slamming into the alien shields. The dreadnaughts, their hulls still bearing the scars of the previous battle, shuddered under the onslaught but pressed forward, their weapons systems flaring to life.

The battle was joined, and the void lit up with the fire of a thousand suns as the two fleets clashed. The *Excalibur* shuddered and bucked, her shields straining under the relentless assault of the alien weapons.

An explosion on the bridge of the *Excalibur* caused tremendous damage. It took me a minute to get his bearings.

I heard a loud, "Dammit!"

It sounded appropriate given the circumstance, but something was not quite right.

The word seemed inappropriate coming from Midshipman Angelica Nicole.

Then I saw her torn body. It was a bloody mess. I was unprepared for the vision. I froze overwhelmed with emotions of grief and sorrow. Before I could recover my composure and go to her aid, Master Chief Kovalen was there like a winged angel lifting her and carrying her to the medics.

I thought, *the real cost of war!*

Even as the battle raged, I could see that our new tactics were having an effect. The concentrated firepower of the human ships, focused on the dreadnaughts' weakened shields, was starting to take its toll. One by one, the massive alien ships began to falter, their hulls breached and their systems failing.

"Fighter squadrons, commence attack run!" I ordered, his eyes blazing with fierce determination. "Target the damaged dreadnaughts and take them out of the fight!"

The fighter-bombers, sleek and deadly, surged forward, their weapons systems primed and ready. They darted through the chaos of the battle, weaving and dodging the enemy fire with a grace that belied their deadly purpose.

As they closed in on the wounded dreadnaughts, the fighter-bombers unleashed a devastating barrage of missiles and plasma fire, their weapons tearing through the weakened shields and ripping into the enemy hulls.

One by one, the dreadnaughts began to fall. Their massive forms were consumed by the brilliant flare of exploding power cores. Once an invincible force, the alien fleet began to waver, their resolve crumbling in the face of the human onslaught.

On the bridge of the *Excalibur*, I watched as the tide of battle turned.

"All ships, press the attack!" I commanded, my voice ringing across the fleet.

As the last of the enemy ships ran away, the bridge of the *Excalibur* erupted in cheers.

My face was lined with exhaustion, but my eyes remained bright with triumph. Sagging back into my command chair, a soft sigh escaping my lips.

We've done it, against all odds.

After the battle, the damaged ships limped back to Janus, struggling to repair their systems and treat the many wounded. Among them was Midshipman Angelica Nicole, who had suffered severe injuries during the intense fighting.

Nicole's body was a tapestry of burns and wounds, the explosions having taken a heavy toll on her young frame. Several of her internal organs had ruptured, requiring hours of delicate surgery to reconstruct. Oxygen conduits, blood tubes, and electrical wires snaked across her body, connecting to her mouth, nose, and veins. These lifelines allowed a steady stream of chemicals and nano-bots to flow through her blood and endocrine systems, working tirelessly to revitalize her damaged tissues and give her a fighting chance at survival.

Inside Nicole's body, the nano-bots embarked on a microscopic journey, conducting preprogrammed surgeries and cellular repairs with precision and efficiency. Electrical sensors, wired to her temples, monitored her brain functions, while others kept a watchful eye on her heart and lungs. The surgeon, with steady hands and a determined focus, performed skin grafts and cut away the dead tissue ravaged by radiation burns. It was a painstaking process, but one that ultimately succeeded in keeping Nicole alive.

As she lay in the regeneration chamber, Nicole listened to the bustling activity around her. The chatter of the crew, discussing their impending arrival at Janus and their plans for liberty, filled the air. Despite her weakened state, her body held together by long swatches of sutures, Nicole yearned to join them, to be up and about once more. Even the slightest movement sent waves of pain through her healing body, but her spirit remained undaunted.

Amidst the background noise, Nicole caught the mutterings of the med techs discussing the doctor attending to her. The room fell oddly quiet when Master Chief Kovalenko entered, a chuckle escaping his lips as he approached her bedside.

"Begging your pardon, Chief, I don't see anything to laugh about," Nicole grumbled, shifting uncomfortably in the regeneration chamber.

Kovalenko's smile only broadened. "Of course, young one," he said, his tone light. "There's nothing at all to laugh about."

"Then kindly remove that grin," Nicole retorted, her brow furrowing. "And don't call me that."

"Anything else?" Kovalenko asked, pulling his face into an exaggerated scowl, though the corners of his mouth twitched with barely contained amusement.

"No," Nicole huffed, her frustration evident.

"Then I'll get back to my duties," Kovalenko said, giving her a nod before turning to leave.

Left alone once more, Nicole swore under her breath. She had intended to ask the Chief about the ship's condition, but the opportunity had slipped away. Even confined to the regeneration chamber, Nicole detested inactivity, loathed being kept in the dark about the goings-on aboard the ship.

Her thoughts were interrupted by the arrival of a med-tech, bearing a variety of fruits. "Captain's compliments," the petty officer said, setting a basket down beside her. "He thought you'd like to know, we're approaching Janus."

"Please pass my thanks on to the captain," Nicole replied, a flicker of gratitude warming her heart.

As the petty officer departed, Nicole reached for a piece of soft fruit, savoring the sweet juices that burst onto her tongue with each bite. She paused mid-chew, however, when the sound of the captain's voice drifted in from outside her room.

Moments later, the doctor entered, I was at his side. The doctor's critical gaze swept over Nicole, assessing her condition with practiced efficiency.

"I'm sure you've seen worse than me?" Nicole queried, a hint of defiance in her tone.

The doctor shook his head. "No, actually. You have significant injuries, though the med team has done excellent work on you. You're on the mend, but I'm sorry, I need to examine you more thoroughly."

As he touched her sensitive body, Nicole yelled, "Dammit!"

Then she let loose a string of invectives that would have made Master Chief Kovalenko proud.

The doctor's expression remained impassive.

"I'll give you something for the pain, but you'll have to manage that foul temper yourself."

CHAPTER 33

Lionheart

The mess hall was a sea of exhausted faces and bandaged bodies. The adrenaline of battle was replaced by the bone-deep weariness of survival. But beneath the fatigue was an undercurrent of something else—a buzzing energy of triumph.

Ayne Chalamet slumped into a chair on the *Excalibur*. "I can't believe we made it," she said, her voice a mix of wonder and disbelief.

Horatio Chen nodded. His eyes investigated the distance. "It was like something out of a legend. The way Captain Thorne just...charged right into the thick of it."

"I thought he'd lost his mind," Steadman admitted. "Going head-to-head with those behemoths? It seemed like suicide."

Lieutenant Stamos shook his head. "But it wasn't, was it? Somehow, he knew."

Master Chief Kovalenko leaned forward, his grizzled face etched with a newfound respect. "I've never experienced anything like it. The way he maneuvered the *Excalibur*, the twists and turns, the countermeasures...it was like a dance."

His young face still flushed with the heat of battle; William Craig spoke up. "Do you think he planned it? Or was it just guesswork?"

Chalamet shrugged, then winced again at the motion. "With the SOS, who knows? They're trained for the impossible, to see patterns and opportunities where the rest of us see noise."

"Well, whatever it was, it saved the fleet," Steadman said. "I'll never doubt Thorne again, that's for sure."

A murmur of agreement rippled around the table. They had all had their doubts, their reservations about the enigmatic captain. But now?

Now, they had seen him in action, the brilliance and the bravery that had earned him his reputation.

Kovalenko sighed, his gaze turning to the viewport. "We're not out of the woods yet. The *Excalibur* laid down a marker. We have got a lot of work to prepare her for another round with those aliens. I have a feeling there are a lot more of them."

Chen nodded, his jaw tightening. "Those aliens, they're not going just to let this go. They'll be back and in greater numbers."

"Then we'll be ready," Craig said, his voice ringing with a determination that belied his youth. "We've got the best crew in the fleet and 'Lionheart' to lead us."

Thorne's nickname, 'Lionheart' hung in the air,

a promise of hope and victory.

In the span of this battle, Elias Thorne had transcended from enigma to legend in the eyes of his crew. His deeds were etched into the fabric of the fleet.

Chalamet smiled a fierce, proud grin. "Damn right. And we'll follow Lionheart to the ends of the universe if that's what it takes."

CHAPTER 34

Mockingbird

The *Excalibur's* briefing room was dimly lit. The only source of illumination come from the holographic display in the center of the table. Commander Varek sat hunched over a stack of papers, his brow furrowed in concentration as he pored over the notes he had meticulously compiled. The room was silent save for the soft hum of the ship's engines and the occasional beep of a console.

Varek's ice-blue eyes, usually sharp and calculating, were now bloodshot from countless hours of research. His once-immaculate uniform was rumpled, the collar loosened in a rare display of informality. He had spent weeks gathering evidence, piecing together a damning case against the enigmatic Captain Thorne.

The hiss of the door sliding open broke Varek's concentration. He looked up to see me striding into the room, my shoulders filling out the crisp lines of my uniform. My hazel eyes met Varek's gaze with a mixture of curiosity and wariness.

"You asked to see me, Commander?" I asked, my voice resonating in the confined space.

Varek stood, his tall frame unfolding from the chair like a coiled spring. He straightened his spine as he faced the captain. "Yes, I did. We have matters to discuss, Captain Thorne. Or should I even call you that?"

My eyebrows shot up, a flicker of surprise crossing my features. "I beg your pardon?"

Varek gestured to the stack of papers on the table, a triumphant gleam in his eyes. "I've been doing some digging, Thorne. And what I've found is quite interesting. Inconsistencies in your records, gaps in your history, and a series of actions that don't align with your supposed rank and background."

My jaw clenched, a muscle twitching beneath the tanned skin of my cheek. I took a step closer to the table, my gaze falling on the papers. "And what exactly are you implying, Varek?"

Varek's lips curled into a humorless smile. "I'm not implying anything, Thorne. I'm stating facts. Facts that paint a very troubling picture of a man with secrets. Secrets that could be construed as treason against the Imperium."

My eyes narrowed, my posture shifting subtly into a defensive stance. "Treason? That's a serious accusation, Commander. One that I hope you have substantial evidence to back up."

Varek tapped the stack of papers, his long fingers drumming against the surface. "Oh, I have evidence. Months of it. Every inconsistency, every unexplained action, every deviation from protocol from before and during your command of *Excalibur*. It's all here, Thorne. And it's damning."

My hand clenched into a fist at my side, the tendons standing out beneath the skin. "You're treading on dangerous ground, Varek. I am an SOS captain, with a record of service and loyalty that speaks for itself."

Varek scoffed, a harsh sound in the stillness of the room. "Service and loyalty? To whom, Thorne? To the Imperium, or to your own hidden agenda?"

My eyes flashed with anger, a fire burning behind the hazel depths. I took a step forward, my tall frame looming over Varek. "My agenda, Commander, is the safety and security of the Imperium. Every action I have taken, every decision I have made, has been in service of that goal."

Varek held his ground, his chin lifted in defiance. "Then explain the discrepancies, Thorne. Explain the secrets and the lies. If you're as loyal as you claim, you should have nothing to hide."

My jaw worked, a vein pulsing in my temple. For a long moment, I was silent, the tension stretching between us like a taut wire. Finally, I spoke, my voice low and controlled. "I am an SOS officer, Varek. My work often requires secrecy and discretion. There are things I cannot explain, not even to you."

Varek's eyes gleamed with triumph. "Ah, so you admit it. You have secrets, things you're hiding from the chain of command."

My gaze hardened and my posture straightened as I drew myself up to my full height. "I admit nothing, Commander. My deeds speak for themselves. The success of our missions, the lives saved, the enemies defeated. That is my record, and it is one I stand behind with pride."

Varek's fingers tightened on the papers, the edges crinkling beneath his grip. "Be that as it may, Thorne, I have a duty to report my findings to Imperium Command. They will decide if your actions warrant further investigation, or worse, arrest."

My lips thinned, a dangerous glint showed in my eyes. "And I have a duty to warn you, Varek, that making false accusations against an SOS officer is a serious offense. One that carries the penalty of death."

Varek's face paled slightly, a flicker of uncertainty crossing his sharp features. "Are you threating me, Thorne?"

I shook my head, a mirthless smile tugging at the corner of his mouth. "Not a threat, Commander. A reminder. The Imperium values loyalty and honor above all else. To make baseless claims against one of its most elite officers is to invite their wrath."

Varek swallowed hard, a bead of sweat trickling down his temple. He glanced at the papers, suddenly unsure of the strength of his case. The weight of Thorne's gaze bore down on him, the intensity of the captain's presence filling the room like a physical force.

For a long moment, we stared at each other, the air crackling with tension. Finally, Varek broke the silence, his voice strained. "I will consider your words carefully, Thorne. But know that I will not be intimidated into silence. If there is treachery afoot, I will uncover it, no matter the cost."

I inclined my head, a gesture of acknowledgment rather than agreement. "As you say, Commander. But be certain of your evidence before you make any accusations. The consequences of being wrong are steep indeed. And you will address me as Captain and Sir, in the future. Is that clear?"

"Aye aye, sir."

Varek sank back into his chair, his heart pounding in his chest. He stared at the papers before him, suddenly uncertain of his next move. The specter of death hung over him, a stark reminder of the power and influence wielded by the SOS.

But beneath the fear, a spark of determination still burned. Varek knew he could not let this matter rest, not until he had uncovered the truth behind Thorne's secrets.

No matter the cost.

CHAPTER 35

Cliffhanger

On the bridge of *Excalibur,* I stood before the vast viewscreen, my eyes fixed on the planet Janus. Behind me, the crew worked with quiet efficiency, their voices low and focused as they monitored the ship's systems.

My thoughts drifted to Kate, to the memory of our parting. I wondered if she was waiting for me on Janus. The pain of her absence was a dull ache in my chest, a constant companion in the long hours of his duty. But I pushed the feeling aside, focusing instead on the task at hand—the reinforcement ships that had just arrived.

The viewscreen flickered with a recorded message from Admiral Collins. The older man's face was lined with fatigue, his eyes shadowed by the weight of command.

"Captain Thorne," Collins began, his voice grave. "I have new orders for you and the *Excalibur.*"

Collins's expression darkened, his brow

furrowing. "We've received disturbing reports from Cygni about the aliens at Kruger."

My pulse quickened, a sense of foreboding settling in his gut.

Collins shook his head, his eyes troubled. "We need you to find out more about the aliens. The Imperium Command has ordered a reinforcement task force to investigate. It will reach Cygni with this message. I want you to lead it."

My eyes widened, surprise and trepidation warred within me.

Me?

Collins said, "You've proven yourself time and again, Thorne. Your actions in the Cygni system have shown that you have the skills and the courage to face the unknown. Command believes you're the right man for the job."

I swallowed hard, the weight of the responsibility settling on my shoulders like a physical burden. I glanced around the bridge, taking in the faces of my crew. They looked to me with trust and expectation, ready to follow me into the very jaws of hell if I asked it of them.

I turned back to the viewscreen, my jaw set with determination.

The Admiral's face grew somber, his voice heavy with implication. "But be warned, Thorne. There may be more enemies out there than we know."

Collins's image flickered; the recording began to break up. "Godspeed, Captain Thorne. The fate of the Imperium may well rest on your shoulders."

With a final nod, the Admiral's face vanished, replaced once more by the starfield. I started, my mind racing with the implications of the mission before me, but I knew that the *Excalibur* would never back down from a fight. No matter how high the stakes, or how great the cost.

CHAPTER 36

It's Complicated

A month later, I stood before Kate in the blooming gardens of the Janus settlement.

I took a shaky breath. Every time I looked at her, I saw a woman with joy in her eyes and love in her heart.

She touched my arm.

"Elias," her voice was soft, laced with worry, "Are you alright?"

"Yes," I said, but the word burned in my throat. To be Elias Thorne, the Lionheart, had been both shield and burden. Now, it was an inescapable trap.

I am living a lie! She deserves the truth.

Yet the truth might destroy everything.

I choked out, "There are... complications. My past... is catching up with me."

I cast my eyes down.

Kate's fingers cupped my chin, tilting my face back towards her. "Elias, we can't build a future on secrets."

I closed my eyes.

I whispered, "You deserve more."

But Kate did not recoil. Instead, a determined glint shone in her eyes. "What I deserve is the man I love," she said. "Titles and accolades mean nothing. Show me who you truly are."

The world seemed to tilt.

Does she mean it?

I steeled myself to confess.

It was beyond reckless, beyond foolish, and yet it was utterly necessary.

"I'm not Elias Thorne," I exclaimed. The words fell like heavy stones.

A frown creased her lovely brow. "No? You are not Lionheart?"

"No," he choked out, the full weight of the confession almost crushing him.

Her frown deepened. Her expression clouded by confusion.

She said, "I don't understand."

I braced for her outburst.

Then, her hands settled on my chest. "It doesn't change who you are," she said, her voice low but unwavering. "What's in a name? Titles did not win battles or save us from enemies. You did. If this name is our problem. Then choose another."

A long moment passed.

Then, I said, "I'm Ethan Hawk, a third-class sailor caught in a lie that spiraled out of control. I deceived everyone, including you."

Her shock showed on her face.

She struggled to comprehend.

Then, her smile returned with a touch of sympathy. "We all wear masks sometimes. Mine was a lab coat, the shield of a scientist."

Surprisingly, hope returned to me.

She continued, "Love... love strips masks away. It shows us the messy, flawed, confused beings' underneath."

She leaned in. I met her halfway. Our kiss fueled our desire and the promise of acceptance. She placed her hands in mine, her gaze steady and sure. "Leave the past behind, Ethan Hawk. Let's build our future together."

In that moment, the borrowed name of Elias Thorne fell away like a discarded cloak. With Kate, perhaps ... just perhaps, I could forge a future worthy of the woman who saw not my title but the fire in my lion heart.

-    the end   -

FROM THE AUTHOR

I hope you enjoyed this book. I must confess that I am proud of my characters and the stories they tell. Ethan is bold and brave, with an intense sense of responsibility—qualities I admire. I would be grateful if you could post your comments and reviews on Amazon. Any feedback you provide on the new characters in the series would be helpful.

Regards,

H. Peter Alesso

For notifications of future books, click the Follow button on the author page.

Coming Soon!

Book #2 *By Any Other Means*

When reinforcements arrive at Janus, Ethan Hawk is stunned when the real Elias Thorne confronts him.

Thorne is undercover and wants Ethan to continue with the deception. Thorne explains that he has been on a covert mission investigating a revolutionary faction within the Imperium. He believes that Ethan's unique position could be valuable in uncovering the truth.

Kate Haliday's groundbreaking research into dark matter turns dangerous when she uncovers a conspiracy threatening to destabilize the Imperium. As Kate and Ethan work together to unravel the mystery, they find themselves drawn into a web of political intrigue and betrayal that tests their trust in each other and their belief in the cause they have sworn to defend.

Ethan must navigate the complex dynamics with Commander Varek, who is suspicious. The alien invasion of the Krug remains a constant threat to the space fleet and the galactic empire.

Made in United States
North Haven, CT
04 September 2024

56925911R10131